'How dare you

The coolly bro
a flagrantly m
mouth tightene
be in charge are
Sam Ryker, and I was expecting a Dr George
Maxwell.' His frowning gaze swept over her
and there was a glint in the startlingly blue
eyes that might have been intimidating if she
weren't so angry.

'*I'm* Dr Maxwell, Dr *Georgia* Maxwell.'

Dear Reader

In Caroline Anderson's ONCE MORE, WITH FEELING, Emily and David meet again after their divorce, in HEART ON THE LINE Jean Evans's Georgia goes to Ethiopia after a broken engagement, and in Australia Meredith Webber's Elly has A DIFFERENT DESTINY. We're very pleased to introduce new author Josie Metcalfe, whose Rebecca and Alex have NO ALTERNATIVE but to respond to each other. With such good reading, how could you not have a wonderful Christmas? Enjoy!

The Editor

!!!STOP PRESS!!! If you enjoy reading these medical books, have you ever thought of writing one? We are always looking for new writers for LOVE ON CALL, and want to hear from you. Send for the guidelines, with SAE, and start writing!

Jean Evans was born in Leicester and married shortly before her seventeenth birthday. She has two married daughters and several grandchildren. She gains valuable information and background for her medical romances from her husband, who is a senior nursing administrator. She now lives in Hampshire, close to the New Forest, and within easy reach of the historic city of Winchester.

Recent titles by the same author:

THE FRAGILE HEART
A DANGEROUS DIAGNOSIS

HEART ON
THE LINE

BY
JEAN EVANS

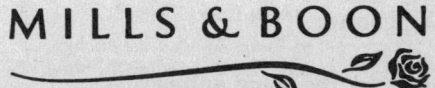

MILLS & BOON

MILLS & BOON LIMITED
ETON HOUSE, 18-24 PARADISE ROAD
RICHMOND, SURREY TW9 1SR

For Simon,
with love

*MILLS & BOON, the Rose Device and LOVE ON CALL
are trademarks of the publisher.*

*First published in Great Britain 1994
by Mills & Boon Limited*

© *Jean Evans 1994*

*Australian copyright 1994   Philippine copyright 1994
This edition 1994*

ISBN 0 263 78884 9

*Set in Times 11 on 12½ pt. by
Rowland Phototypesetting Limited,
Bury St Edmunds, Suffolk*

03-9412-39928

Made and printed in Great Britain

CHAPTER ONE

GEORGIA MAXWELL woke slowly, shivering in the cold of an African dawn. Her mouth felt dry and, for a few seconds, as she jerked fully back to consciousness, she couldn't remember where she was.

A brief glance at her watch showed that she must have slept for nearly an hour. Blinking hard, she turned stiffly to look out of the window just as the small plane banked sharply over the deep rift-valley below. Then she remembered, gasping involuntarily as the thin veil of early morning mist broke and she caught her first real glimpse of the beauty below.

So this was Ethiopia, spread like the wings of a giant butterfly, caught and held between Sudan to the north and the desert plains of Kenya to the east.

She jumped as the pilot leaned across, resting a hand on her arm. Grinning, Dave Farrell raised his voice to make himself heard above the noise of the engines.

'It seemed a shame to wake you. You were sleeping like a baby. We'll be coming in to land in about ten minutes.' He nodded in the direction of the ground where sunlight shimmered on the surface of the water. 'I figured you'd want to take a look. You'll see quite a few lakes in this area. Some of them are fresh water, others brackish, depending on the source.'

Tucking a strand of honey-blonde hair behind her ear, Georgia gazed down at the scene below and felt her pulse-rate quicken as the rays of the fast rising sun ignited the slopes with the colour of molten gold. Seen from the air the vastness of the continent and its infinite variations, the change from arid desert to lush green slopes, falling away to the valley floor, filled her with a sense of excitement that banished every last scrap of tiredness.

Craning her neck, she said, 'I can see a river.'

Dave followed the direction of her gaze and nodded. 'That'll be the Awash. It runs north along the rift until it peters out in a salt lake somewhere on the plain.'

She nodded, staring out of the window as the ground seemed gradually to come closer, feeling her body respond with a sudden surge of adrenalin.

Not that she was a stranger to travel. It was in her blood. As a child whose father had been an army surgeon, she had developed a feeling of wanderlust at an early age, had been given the opportunity to see places most people only ever dreamed about. But never Africa.

Africa had been her own private dream. She had read about it, been fascinated by its vastness, its wildlife and its people for as long as she could remember. But nothing she had read or learned about it had quite prepared her for the reality. She turned to the young American sitting beside her.

'How long have you been out here?'

'At Batandi? About eighteen months.' He checked the altimeter.

The sun was coming up fast, the chill of the morning already giving a promise of the heat that was to come. Georgia peered at her reflection in the window, briefly raking a hand through the swath of her long, blonde hair. Even tied back as it now was, the weight of it seemed to tug at her scalp, making her head ache. Or was it the sudden, unexpected rush of nervous tension? It wasn't every day you gave up a way of life, travelled to the other side of the world to work with people you'd never met. What would they be like?

Her green eyes clouded slightly. What did she really know about conditions out here except what she, like millions of people, had read about in the Press or seen on television? She flexed her shoulders in an attempt to ease the tension. 'I've heard a lot about the way things were out here. Have things changed? Has there been any improvement?'

Dave pulled a wry face. 'There are too many natural enemies. Disease, drought, famine. You

name it, these people know all about it. If the
rains come and they get a good harvest it's a good
year, but it might be followed by three bad ones.'

Georgia reached for a Thermos of ice-cold
juice, poured a cup, proffering it to the fair-haired
American. He took it, drinking greedily before
passing it back. 'But it doesn't ever make you feel
you want to give up?' she enunciated.

His tanned features broke into a grin. 'I've been
accused of having a stubborn streak,' he bellowed.
'I guess it helps.'

Smiling, she refilled the cup, savouring the cool
liquid. It still seemed impossible that only a few
days ago she had been in London, a very wet,
cold London, in a busy accident and emergency
department at one of the large teaching hospitals
to be precise, doing her best to stay awake after
a solid sixty-hour stint on duty.

'There must be easier ways of earning a living?'

He tapped the fuel gauge. 'I forgot to mention,
I've also got a low boredom threshold. No, seriously, I love the work. Your big city hospitals are
fine but they aren't for me.' He glanced in her
direction. 'At the risk of sounding corny, how
about you? What's a nice girl like you doing in a
place like this?'

Georgia smiled. 'It was all pretty boring really.
I saw an advertisement in the international aid
organisation's journal. The idea of a sort of
African flying doctor service intrigued me. I'd

completed my year as a houseman.' She frowned. 'I wasn't sure quite where I was going next. Oh, I've nothing against general practice, I just didn't feel it was right for me, not yet anyway. Maybe in a few years' time.'

'So you decided to make a break for it?'

'Right.' Her generous mouth curved into a smile. 'The advertisement seemed almost like the answer to a prayer. I felt I needed a new challenge. I applied and the rest, as they say, is history.'

'Well, you certainly picked the right place. One thing we can guarantee out here, you work, you get exhausted, frustrated maybe, but never bored.' His American accent seemed to deepen. 'I take it there aren't any ties? No boyfriend lurking in the background?'

'No, no ties.' She stared out of the window.

'It's probably just as well.' Dave's concentration was centred on the instruments as, almost imperceptibly, the drone of the engines changed slightly. 'This place has enough problems to keep you going full time, without bringing in any from outside.'

Georgia drew her gaze away from the window to look at him. 'I gather you're concentrating on a major immunisation programme at the moment? I hadn't realised measles was such a problem.'

'It's one of the biggest killers out here, that and diarrhoea. That's one of the reasons I was in

Addid, apart from collecting you, that is. I was picking up an emergency consignment of vaccines and other medical supplies, not to mention the odd food parcel and the latest mail drop.'

He reached out, flicking a switch, bringing the radio crackling to life. 'Flying Doctor One to Batandi Base. Are you receiving, over?'

A voice cut through the static. 'Receiving you loud and clear, Flying Doctor One. Go ahead, Dave. Nice to have you back with us. I hope you brought the goodies, including our relief. We need him, mate.'

'Goodies all safe and sound——' Dave's brown eyes studied Georgia appreciatively '—and definitely in good shape, though I suspect the chief may be in for something of a shock. ETA about five minutes, by the way.'

There was a chuckle from the other end. 'I'll pass on your message to Sam. Over and out.'

Dave flicked the switch. 'That was Mike Richards, our radio operator.'

Georgia nodded, straightening her shoulders and easing the muscles. 'I can't wait to meet everyone.'

'They're a good team. We couldn't do the job we do if they weren't. Out here you tend to depend on each other. Sam is pretty keen on everyone pulling their weight.'

She glanced in his direction. 'Sam?'

'Sam Ryker, the chief.'

'Oh, I thought you were in charge.'

His laugh shattered her illusions. 'Lord, no. I'm afraid I'm one of the lesser mortals. Doctor, bacteriologist, you name it, I do it. That's another thing you'll learn pretty quickly out here—to adapt.' His gaze swept over her. 'Don't worry, you'll soon get used to it.' His mouth twitched. 'Whether I can say the same for Sam is another matter.'

Georgia felt her heart give a sharp thud. 'I don't understand. I was told a relief doctor was needed urgently.'

'Sure, that's right.' Dave frowned. 'Geoff Patricks, who set up the mission hospital out here about ten years ago, had a heart attack about three months back. Sam had been with him for a while so it was natural that he took over. He'd been doing most of the work anyway. Geoff's health had been going steadily downhill for some time, but he was a stubborn old devil, wouldn't give in. But then we started to get a few doses of measles; within a week they were coming in thick and fast. There was no way we could cope with the intake of new patients, carry out the immunisations and still run the clinics.'

'Yes, I can see it would be a problem.'

'I guess that's why Sam's been a shade edgy of late. Don't get me wrong, he's a brilliant doctor, but he's responsible for the whole programme since they flew Geoff out. I guess you could say we're still here on sufferance. If the project can't be seen to be working. . .' he shrugged '. . .we get the heave-ho. It's a sad fact, but everything comes down to cash in the end. Funds only stretch so far. So, the chief doesn't take kindly to disruptions.'

Georgia stifled a tiny feeling that she was going to have trouble liking Dr Sam Ryker. 'Which is presumably why I'm here, to help ease the pressure.' She frowned. For a second there she could have sworn she detected a faint gleam of laughter in the American's brown eyes as he turned to look at her, and wondered why it should fill her with a sense of foreboding. 'So what's the problem?'

He grinned. 'No problem, no problem at all. Like I said, we need all the help we can get.'

So why, she couldn't help wondering as the small plane bumped down gently and came slowly to a halt in a cloud of dust on the bumpy, man-made runway, did she get the distinct impression that he wasn't entirely telling the truth?

'It's OK, you can open your eyes now.' Dave touched her arm lightly, pointing ahead. 'There we are. Home, for the next few months anyway.'

She followed his direction and wasn't sure whether it was relief or trepidation she felt as she climbed stiffly out of the small aircraft.

Reaching for her bag, she set it down. So this was Batandi. It was unlike anything she had imagined. Built into the hillside, several of the buildings were little more than a roof on supports beneath which stood a table and a couple of canvas chairs. Others were long wooden bungalows with verandas and it was from one of these that a slim figure in cool white cotton jeans and a short-sleeved shirt, its collar open, exposing tanned skin, emerged, her naturally wavy, dark hair tied back in a ponytail.

She was young but, as she came hurrying down the steps to greet them, Georgia realised that she was more than the eighteen or nineteen which had been her first impression. She was attractive and her figure was certainly that of a woman.

'Hi,' she greeted Dave as he unloaded packages from the plane. 'I'm glad you're back. You made good time.'

'Problems?' He reached for the mail bag, dumping it on the ground.

'You could say. That trickle of measles cases we had in last week has turned into a torrent. We've had twenty new cases in the past thirty-six hours.'

Dave's mouth hardened. 'That sounds like trouble.'

'I'd say so, and some of the latest batch have a few cases of serious malnutrition thrown in. Sam has already given them the once-over and started treatment. They'll stay here, of course, until we're as sure as we can be that they're going to make it, but it's beginning to look as if we were right.

I'd say we're in for a full-scale epidemic, and it's not localised. Some of the mothers have walked for days to bring their children in.'

Dave turned to the plane again, unloading a couple of insulated boxes which he handed to her. 'In that case you'll be extra glad of these.'

'The vaccines. You're a life-saver.'

'Let's hope so.'

Georgia saw the grim look that passed between them. 'I seem to have arrived at a bad moment.'

The girl's smile was at once friendly and full of apology. 'Oh, lor, look, I'm sorry. I didn't mean to be rude. I should have introduced myself before launching into an account of our troubles. I'm Jan, Jan Reid, senior sister, and you must be. . .' Her amused glance went from Georgia to the American. 'I take it you *are* our relief?' Her hand came out to grasp Georgia's.

'That's right. Georgia Maxwell.'

'You've probably guessed we're more than a little glad to see you. How was the flight?'

'Mostly boring. I must say it's good to be here.'

Jan laughed. 'I'd wait until you've seen what you're letting yourself in for before you say that. You seem to have arrived just in time for a fair old emergency. From a purely selfish point of view it's great to see you, though it hardly seems fair to drop you straight in at the deep end, before you've even had time to unpack.'

'That's what I'm here for,' Georgia smilingly

assured her. 'I can't wait to get started.'

The other girl grinned appreciatively. 'It's not quite that bad, yet. At least you deserve some time to settle in and get your bearings. Look, I've got to take these supplies over to the clinic; why don't I show you to your bungalow at the same time? You can stow your luggage then I'll show you around. Don't worry about the rest of your bags. One of the boys will bring them to your quarters.'

'I'll bring them myself,' Dave volunteered, 'then I'd better go find Sam. I've got a couple of messages and reports to deliver.'

'He'll certainly be glad to see you. He's got his hands full.' To Georgia she said, 'He's taking the first clinic, which is why he wasn't here to meet you, but he sends his apologies and says he'll catch up with you later.' She smiled and, despite Georgia's protests, picked up one of the bags. 'The living accommodation is over here.' She led the way across the compound towards several small bungalows. 'It's fairly basic but I think you'll find it adequate.'

Following her up the steps, Georgia's glance went to a truck, the top covered by canvas.

'That's our emergency vehicle. We keep it at the ready, stocked with supplies, so that if we get a call we can leave straight away.'

'You're certainly well organised.'

'We have to be.' Jan smiled, leading the way

along a small veranda to push open the door. 'Sam may seem a bit of a stickler for efficiency at times, but out here people die of diseases we in the west tend to think of as minor childhood ailments. These people don't have our resistance to them. On top of that there's often drought or any number of other natural hazards, and it's not as if they can just pop down the road to the nearest health centre.' She gave a slight laugh. 'Sorry, I didn't intend giving a lecture but. . .' she nodded towards the compound '. . .hence the truck.'

She led the way into a small room. 'You can see what I mean about it being basic. If it's any consolation we don't get to spend too much time inside.' She put the bag on the bed as Georgia looked round, taking in the small, colourful rug on the floor, a table and a chest of drawers and a tiny wardrobe.

'It's fine,' she pronounced. 'It has everything I'm likely to need.' Once she had unpacked her clothes and the few books she had brought with her, she added to herself.

'Well, I'll leave you to get sorted out.' Jan looked at her watch. 'Oh, lor, I'm supposed to be on the ward. We've got a young mum in labour. It's her first. She's only fourteen and a little nervous.'

'Fourteen!'

Jan smiled. 'You'll get used to it. Out here, fourteen is quite usual. I've seen them younger.

Anyway, look, sort yourself out. There's a shower of sorts through there if you want to freshen up.'

'Mm, I can't wait. Oh, but what about Dr Ryker? Shouldn't I at least. . .?'

'Sam, and no, don't worry about it. I doubt if he'd thank you for interrupting his clinic. I'll see you later.' With a wave she was gone, hurrying down the steps and running across the compound.

Georgia stood for a few seconds, taking in her new surroundings before opening her suitcase. She hung clothes in the wardrobe and her undies she arranged in one of the drawers, the actions helping in some small way to lessen some of the nervousness that suddenly welled up inside her.

After all, she had come here to work and she was good at her job. But it was a long way, a million light-years away, from St Chad's, she found herself thinking as she stepped out of her shoes, easing her toes.

She stared at her reflection in a small mirror and grimaced. She felt hot and sticky. Dust seemed to clog every pore and cling to her hair. Back home it was probably raining, but she wasn't going to think about home. She had wanted a fresh start, a new challenge. Well, this was it. She wasn't going to let herself be defeated by homesickness before she had even finished unpacking.

Reaching for her other bag, she groaned as her muscles protested. Stretching, she freed her hair of its restraining tie, running her fingers through it. She dismissed the idea of changing and going straight across to the hospital. First impressions counted for a lot. She didn't want to meet her new colleagues looking like something the cat had dragged in.

Turning on the shower, she unzipped her skirt and, stepping out of it, began unfastening her shirt. As she did so she tried to build up some kind of mental picture of the man who was to be her boss for the next few months at least. A stickler for efficiency, someone who, she suspected, didn't tolerate fools gladly, a brilliant doctor. Probably quite elderly, she mused as she began to tug her satin slip over her head.

'Dr Maxwell?' Footsteps sounded on the veranda and she cursed under her breath as the delicate material tangled with the clip she had used to secure her hair. 'I'm sorry I wasn't here to meet you when you arrived. I hope the flight. . .'

Tugging frantically at the slip, she heard the male voice exclaim sharply, 'What the hell. . .?'

She felt the hot colour surge into her cheeks as she spun round to see the tall figure standing framed in the doorway. It wasn't just an overwhelming sense of power that seemed to emanate from him as he stood there, it was several seconds before she realised he was studying her slender figure appreciatively, clad only, she realised with a sense of shock, in the briefest of bra and

panties, with an intensity that almost took her
breath away.

She was immediately conscious of every line of
his taut, muscular body, from his shoulders
beneath the open-necked shirt to a slim waist and
lean thighs beneath the faded jeans he was
wearing.

With a gasp of protest she snatched her robe
from the bed, holding it defensively in front of
her. Colour rode high on her cheekbones as she
viewed him through hostile eyes.

'How dare you come barging in like that?
Didn't anyone ever teach you that it's polite to
knock before entering a room? Just who are you
anyway?'

For several seemingly interminable seconds the
coolly brooding gaze subjected her to a flagrantly
masculine appraisal before his mouth tightened
ominously. 'I might ask you the same question. I
just happen to be in charge around here. The
name is Ryker, Sam Ryker, and I was expecting
a Dr George Maxwell.' His frowning gaze swept
over her and there was a glint in the startlingly
blue eyes that might have been intimidating if she
weren't so angry.

'*I'm* Dr Maxwell, Dr *Georgia* Maxwell.'

Blue eyes looked coolly into hers and, for the
first time in her life, her height, at five feet eight
inches, suddenly seemed diminished. His mouth
tightened. 'Either this is someone's idea of a joke,

in which case it's in very poor taste, or there's been some mistake. Whichever it is——' his gaze swept over the small room and her suitcase, still on the bed '—I'll see you in my office in fifteen minutes. Oh, and don't bother to unpack, Dr Maxwell, because you won't be staying.'

CHAPTER TWO

TAKING a deep, controlling breath, Georgia faced the man standing in front of her. 'I can't believe you're serious.' One look at the ruggedly impassive features, however, was sufficient to tell her that there had been no mistake.

A shower had done nothing to take the edge off her embarrassment or her anger, but at least dressed she felt slightly less vulnerable. Not that that was saying much as Sam Ryker motioned her to a chair then remained standing himself.

'I'm sorry you feel that way——' his cool stare flicked over her '—because I assure you I meant every word.'

'But. . .you asked for an emergency medical relief.'

'I'm well aware of what I asked for. It seems I failed to make myself entirely clear. What I asked for was someone with experience of this type of work, someone tough enough to step into my shoes, should the need arise.' His gaze narrowed, raking her slender figure and delicate features in a manner so flagrantly masculine that it almost took her breath away. 'With the best will in the world, Dr Maxwell, I'd say you have a long way to go before you qualify.'

Sam Ryker had to be over six feet tall. His hair was dark, almost black, and, now that she had a chance to study him properly, he was, she realised, not a day over thirty-five, but he had an aura of power. His authority was tangible, underlined in the firm angle of his jaw, the shrewd intelligence behind those blue eyes.

Georgia swallowed hard. 'But that's unfair.' Her eyes flashed. 'Worse, it's nothing short of chauvinism. How dare you make such judgements. . .?'

'Because it's my job,' he said evenly. 'I make judgements every day of my life. Other people's lives depend on it.' His mouth twisted. 'I'm not entirely naïve, Dr Maxwell. I stopped believing in miracles a long time ago. I didn't expect to get everything I asked for, but I did hope that whoever sits behind a desk deciding these things would realise that we're not playing games out here. The last thing I need is someone fresh out of medical school.'

He straightened up and she released a breath she wasn't even aware she had been holding, as if some physical threat had been lifted.

'If I were a man you wouldn't be saying these things. . .'

'You're damn right, because the need wouldn't arise.' He stared at her then turned abruptly away, raking a hand through his hair. 'Look, this isn't personal.'

Georgia made a small sound that might have been a laugh if she hadn't felt so close to tears. 'Well, I've got news for you, Doctor, it *feels* very personal.' She rose to her feet and met his look.

'Tell me, Dr Maxwell, just how old are you?'

She stared at him, feeling her colour rising. 'I'm twenty-seven. Old enough to have completed my training, old enough to have qualified. . .'

'Old enough to have a lover?'

'*What*?' She stared at him, telling herself she must have misunderstood.

'It's a simple enough question. Most women of your age have acquired a boyfriend, husband or lover along the way. I'm asking if you have any ties.'

She drew a breath, a wave of reaction instinctively causing her to clench her fingers. 'I fail to see what my personal life has to do with any of this. How would you respond if I were to ask such personal questions?'

He gave her a curiously bleak smile. 'My marriage isn't the issue here, Doctor, neither is my position.'

Her heart gave a strange little flutter. So he was married. Of course, he would be; he had the kind of looks a lot of women would fall for. She swallowed hard. 'I'm sorry. You're right, of course.'

With a gesture of impatience he turned from the window to face her. 'The people who work out here give a commitment. It's no exaggeration to say that, for the term of their contract, they devote their lives to their work.'

She stiffened. 'Are you saying I have no sense of commitment? Is this another of your totally unfounded judgements? Because if so, let me fill in a few details, Dr Ryker. I qualified four years ago. Since then I've worked in one of the busiest departments in a major training hospital, most recently as registrar. I've dealt with the drunks and fatal accidents. I've dealt with trauma cases. One of the most recent was a child of three who needed a liver transplant. . .'

'Did you find a donor?'

'What?' She frowned. 'No—at least, yes, we found a donor but it was too late, by a matter of couple of hours. Lucy couldn't wait that long. Her parents were with her when she died.'

'You did everything you could.' He gave her a steady look. 'There's always another patient, Doctor. They don't obligingly go away while you grieve. You get on with it. *We* get on with it, and, believe me, death out here is on a scale you've never dreamed of. That's why I have the right to ask questions you may feel squeamish about answering. I demand one hundred and ten per cent of my staff. We're a long way from home, the mail comes through every once in a while, when we can spare the time or someone to fetch it, and provided it hasn't gone missing *en route*. You can't pick up a phone and call home because you're feeling homesick, or because someone metaphorically stepped on your toes.'

She drew in a sharp breath. 'If those things were important to me, I wouldn't be here.'

His mouth twisted. 'I know your type, Dr Maxwell. You may not think it matters but inside a month you'd be crying yourself to sleep, you'd become a liability.'

She faced him, breathing hard. 'I can take care of myself.'

'In the city maybe.'

She closed her eyes briefly in frustration. 'This is pointless. Clearly nothing I can say will make you change your mind. I see no point in pro-longing this conversation.' She gathered up her bag. 'I shall leave as soon as possible.' She was at the door when his voice halted her in her tracks.

'Unfortunately it isn't quite that simple.'

She flung him a scornful look. 'What's the matter, Dr Ryker? Don't tell me you've suddenly developed a conscience? Or have you suddenly realised it might not be so easy, explaining your actions to the organisation's head office? Well, maybe you should have thought of that. . .'

He sighed. 'I've never been afraid to account for my actions. I was making a simple statement of fact.' He straightened up from the desk where he had been half sitting, half standing. 'We don't run a taxi service. We have three methods of transport. You take a train of pack mules and an experienced guide and you walk, maybe for a week, and if you're lucky you may get somewhere. Always supposing, of course, that you don't fall down a ravine or the local *shifta* don't get you first.'

Georgia moistened her suddenly dry lips. '*Sh—shifta*?'

The blue eyes flickered with something disconcertingly like humour. 'The local bandits, and, believe me, I don't recommend a close encounter. You wouldn't find it very savoury. They'd find a woman with your colouring especially exciting.'

'Oh.' She swallowed hard.

'Secondly, we have the plane, which is used strictly for emergencies and bringing in supplies, and, thirdly, we have the trucks, again for emergency use only. We don't have infinite supplies of petrol, Dr Maxwell, and I hate to say it but your departure, desirable though it might be, doesn't count as a priority.'

She gave a short laugh. 'So what do you suggest I do? Walk and take my chances? Perhaps you'd care to point out the road to Addis, since you're so eager to be rid of me.'

'Don't tempt me, Doctor.' The blue eyes contained a definite hint of humour. He straightened up. 'I may not want you here but I have no illusions. We need a doctor and it seems that, until I can make other arrangements, you're it. So it looks as if we're both going to have to be patient.'

It briefly occurred to Georgia that an encounter with the *shifta* could surely be only marginally less attractive than having to stay here where she clearly wasn't welcome.

'And just what do you suggest I do in the meantime? Make the tea?'

He gave a lazy grin and her breath caught in her throat at the sudden realisation that she actually found him sexually attractive. 'You sound like a pretty resourceful creature, Dr Maxwell. I'm sure you'll find something to keep you out of mischief.'

She flung him a look. 'This is impossible. Surely there must be some way of getting me back?'

'Forget it.' His gaze narrowed. 'Even if I could spare the transport, we're up to our necks in an epidemic. I need all the help I can get right now. You're a doctor. As long as you have to remain you can make yourself useful——' He broke off with a gesture of irritation as someone tapped at the door and in response to the curt summons Jan Reid popped her head round the door.

'Sorry, Sam, but you're needed over at the clinic. Oz thinks one of the patients may have a case of onchocerciasis.' She glanced at Georgia.

'It's sometimes called river blindness because it's caused by worms entering the body through a cut, maybe, often in infected water.' Turning back to Sam, she said, 'He'd like your opinion. . .'

'I'm on my way.' Heading for the door, he flung a look in Georgia's direction. 'Don't get too settled. While you're here you may as well earn your keep, but I meant what I said. The first chance I get you're out of here.'

He was gone before she could speak and she stood rooted to the spot, feeling a tide of anger and frustration wash over her.

Jan closed the door, turning uncertainly to Georgia. 'Are you all right?'

'What? Oh, yes, I'm fine. . .I think.' In a weary gesture she flopped into a chair, brushing her hair back as she tried to gather her thoughts into some semblance of order. She had left London full of enthusiasm and excitement, and with a belief that she was actually going to be able to do something worthwhile. It had taken a human steamroller in the form of Sam Ryker to show her just how naïve that belief was.

'What happened?'

'Apart from the fact that I'm the wrong sex, the wrong age and probably the wrong shape?' Georgia managed lightly. 'You tell me.' She rose unsteadily to her feet, gathering her official letter of introduction and a copy of her contract from the desk where Sam had dropped them. 'I get the

distinct impression he was expecting a Dr *George*
Maxwell?'

Jan grinned. 'It's hardly your fault if someone's
typing isn't up to scratch.'

'Maybe not,' Georgia sighed. 'Unfortunately it
seems Dr Ryker has very specific ideas about the
kind of staff he needs. I'm allowed to stay on a
temporary basis, until he can get a replacement.'
She reached for the white coat she had brought
with her, briskly shrugging herself into it. 'In the
meantime perhaps I could take you up on that
offer of a guided tour?' she managed lightly.

Jan frowned. 'Look, I'm sure Sam didn't
mean. . .'

'It's all right. I'd like to get down to work,'
Georgia said truthfully. If she wasn't going to be
allowed to stay, at least she could use the time
she had to prove to Sam Ryker that he was wrong
about her. 'Besides, he's right. The sooner I start
earning my keep, the better for everyone.' Including her own sanity, was the thought that refused
to go away. Damn Sam Ryker. Without her being
aware of it her hands clenched. She had spent
the past eighteen months coming to terms with
Martin's betrayal. She had thought she had suc-
ceeded until, with a few careless words, he had
managed to open up the old wounds.

Jan looked startled by the note of animosity in
her voice. 'Look, I know things don't seem to
have got off to a very good start between you and

Sam, but I'm sure he doesn't mean the things he said. You caught him at a bad moment. Things haven't been easy lately. He's actually very nice and a brilliant doctor. We're lucky to have him.'

Georgia determinedly swept aside a mental image of the ruggedly chiselled features, the smouldering blue gaze and hard jaw. Brilliant doctor, maybe. She could go along with that. Nice was the word she was having trouble with.

'If you don't mind, I think I'll reserve judgement.'

Jan smiled, the whiteness of her teeth emphasised by her tan. 'He'll cool down. It's this epidemic. It's getting to all of us and, unfortunately, we lost a whole consignment of supplies to bandits.' She shrugged. 'It happens. That doesn't mean we get used to it. Apart from that, Geoff's heart attack added to the pressure on everyone.'

'All the more reason for me to start pulling my weight.' Georgia smiled. A small trickle of sweat between her shoulder-blades was already making its presence felt. 'Seriously, though, I'd like to get to know my way around. I haven't been given any specific duties.'

Jan grinned. 'Don't worry about it. No one gets to stand still around here. Give it a week and you'll be wishing you were back home.'

Not a cat in hell's chance, Georgia thought as she followed her new friend out into the brilliant sunshine. She wouldn't give the arrogant Sam Ryker the satisfaction.

'We hold two clinics a day,' Jan explained as they skirted a large group of mainly women with small children, some squatting, others sitting or standing, clutching their *shammas*, the white cotton blanket-type garment most of the Ethiopians wore, heading towards a collection of larger bungalows.

'I noticed one was underway as we arrived. You certainly start early.'

'It's the coolest part of the day. Some of our patients have walked for days to get here. I don't know how some of them make it, they're in such a poor state, yet they never complain.' Jan paused to speak to one of the dark-skinned women who was suckling an infant, her hand flapping away a plague of flies. Her hair was dressed in multitudinous tiny plaits. She looked exhausted and under-nourished and Georgia put her age at about forty, though it was difficult to be sure as the woman drew the *shamma* over her own head and covered the child.

Jan said something in the woman's own language and the woman laughed coyly behind her hand as Jan straightened up and waved goodbye.

Georgia was fascinated. 'You speak the language?'

Jan smiled. 'I get by. I've managed to pick up a few useful phrases of Amharic. The girl's name is Sisi, Sisi B'tandi. She's a Tigrean. I saw her a couple of months ago when we did a routine visit to her village.' Mounting the steps of one of the larger bungalows, Jan pushed open a swing door. 'She's here because she's pregnant.'

Georgia looked at her. 'But. . .the baby she's suckling now can't be more than five months old, six at most. And what about the woman herself? She looks worn out.'

Jan shot her an amused look. 'How old do you think Sisi is?'

'I'm not sure, forty-ish?'

'She's twenty-five.' Jan held open the door leading to the ward, almost colliding with a dark-skinned girl wearing a white dress and with a brightly coloured scarf concealing her short, tightly curled hair. 'Girma, I was just coming to look for you. I'd like you to meet Dr Georgia Maxwell. Dr Maxwell, this is Girma, one of our senior nursing aides.'

The girl smiled, showing even white teeth. 'Dr Maxwell.'

Jan rested a hand on the girl's arm. 'Girma came to Batandi about three years ago, as a patient, and after her treatment she decided to stay on and train as a nurse herself. Now she's one of our most senior nurses. We're very proud of her.' To the girl she said, 'I'm just going to show Dr Maxwell the nursing station, give her a brief run-down on the system we work, then we'll introduce her to the patients. By the way, how is Dena? Has she come round from the anaesthetic yet?'

'Yes, about half an hour ago. She's doing fine.'

'That's good. We'll pop along in a little while.' The girl hurried away and Jan indicated a small, partitioned area at the end of the ward, occupied by a large desk and an ancient filing cabinet. She grinned. 'This is the office. We keep the patients' records in here. We have forty beds on this particular ward and the turn-over is constant. As one patient is discharged another is admitted.'

'What happens if you get an emergency?'

Jan extracted several files from the cabinet, pushing the drawer to a close. 'We do our best to find a space, but most of these cases are classed as urgent. Most of them come in suffering from conditions that should have been treated months if not years ago, but have been neglected simply because the patient lived too far from a hospital to get the treatment they need. By the time they get to us, what might have been fairly mild has become a chronic condition. Obviously, everyone who comes for treatment will be seen by a doctor who assesses the level of urgency. Those who don't require immediate surgery will simply wait. They know we'll feed them.' She smiled. 'Don't worry, you'll soon get the hang of it.'

Georgia gave a slight laugh. 'I'll take your word for it. You were telling me about Sisi.'

'In fact, Sisi is a typical example of the cases we get. Look, let's go on to the ward and you'll see what I mean. Ah, and here's someone else you should meet.' She greeted the short, stocky man in a white coat. 'Mamdouh, this is Dr Georgia Maxwell, our relief. Georgia, Dr Mamdouh Ozikwe.'

'Doctor.'

They shook hands. Mamdouh Ozikwe was a Nigerian, aged, Georgia guessed, about fifty, with a shock of wispy hair rising from the centre of his balding head. His ebony face wreathed into a smile.

'Dr Maxwell, it is good to see you.'

'Please, call me Georgia.'

'I will do that, if you call me Oz.' He chuckled. 'It's what I'm used to. These people have no respect.'

'I'm showing Georgia round, giving her an idea of what goes on here.'

'Ah, in that case you can't do better than begin here. My apologies, however, I have a clinic, but I shall see you later, at dinner maybe?'

'I shall look forward to it.'

He bustled away and Jan smiled. 'He's nice, a good doctor. He trained in Britain and came out here about a year ago.' Jan paused, unclipping a chart from the end of the first bed. Passing it to Georgia, she glanced at the patient, a young girl who was sleeping, huddled beneath a sheet. 'This is Tashi. She was admitted a week ago and operated on early this morning. She seems to be doing nicely.'

Georgia scanned the notes and moved to the side of the bed. She looked down at the girl, automatically checking her pulse, and said softly, 'She looks very young.'

Jan nodded. 'She's fifteen.'

Georgia flipped a page, frowning over the notes. 'I see she had a fistula repair, a fistula of the bladder caused by. . .' Her gaze rose. 'Caused by prolonged labour in childbirth.'

'That's right.'

'Shocked, Dr Maxwell? You'd better get used to it. You'll find there's a whole new set of values out here.'

Georgia experienced a sense of shock as she realised that her early-warning system, that nervous tingle that ran down her spine, had betrayed her as she turned slowly to see Sam standing there.

Jan looked at her watch. 'Whoops! I'm due to assist in Theatre in an hour. Do you mind if I leave you to it? Will you be all right?' She flung a look at Georgia as she headed for the door.

'I think you can safely leave Dr Maxwell to me.' Sam Ryker's blue eyes flickered briefly over Georgia before he glanced at the sleeping patient, briefly studying the notes before returning the chart to the end of the bed.

'I take it you've seen fistula cases before?'

'Yes, of course, though admittedly not usually in someone so young.'

'Unfortunately, Tashi isn't an exception out here, she's the rule. It isn't unusual for girls to marry and start producing children at the age of thirteen. They may have ten or more pregnancies. Some will end in a miscarriage, some are stillbirths, others stand a good chance of dying within the first three years of life.' His voice held a brief note of bitterness which shocked her.

She looked up to find him watching her. She swallowed hard. 'All right, so I was shocked. I admit it. But that makes me human, it doesn't make me incompetent.' Her gaze rose to challenge his. 'In spite of what you seem to think, I didn't come out here expecting a home from home. I realised things would be different, but I'm willing to learn, given the chance.'

His mouth twisted. 'Unfortunately I don't have time to play nursemaid.'

'I'm not asking you to.'

'You're suggesting I just let you loose? I'm not sure that would be such a good idea.'

Her eyes flashed. 'I came here to work. If I'm not to be allowed to do that then I may as well stay away.' She was heading for the door when his hand on her arm brought her to a halt.

Blue eyes regarded her with an unreadable expression. Only a slight tremor at the corner of his mouth suggested that he was amused. 'Tell me, are you always this fiery?'

Colour surged into her cheeks. 'Only under extreme provocation.' Furiously she tried to break free only to feel his grip tighten.

'And I do seem to have a knack of upsetting you, don't I?'

'I'm not accustomed to having my competence called into question.'

'I wasn't aware that that was what I was doing.'

She met his gaze directly. 'This is getting us nowhere. It's obvious we can never work together.'

His brows drew together in a frown. 'Will it help if I apologise?'

She stared at him, noting for the first time the tiny lines of exhaustion etched around his eyes and mouth. She sensed that, while Sam Ryker may be hard on those around him, he was no less hard on himself. 'I. . .I beg your pardon?'

His mouth tightened. 'We got off to a bad start. You caught me at a bad moment. I've been trying to cover for Geoff. If it hadn't been for this damned epidemic we might have coped, but that's not your fault. I'm sorry. You just happened to bear the brunt of it.'

Georgia licked her dry lips. 'So. . .what exactly are you suggesting?'

His mouth twisted. 'To start with, you could

try calling me Sam. We don't go in much for formalities out here.'

She tested the sound and found it surprisingly pleasant. 'OK, Sam, so—let me be sure I understand this—you're saying I can stay?'

Blue eyes met hers. 'What I'm saying is that for as long as we do have to work together we can at least try to make the best of it. I'm sure we're both adult enough to cope with that, aren't you, George?'

Her heart gave a tiny hiccup, then she remembered the absent Mrs Ryker. 'The name is Georgia,' she ground out, watching his retreating figure, and saw him raise a hand in acknowledgement.

It was only later as she climbed wearily into bed that she began to realise that her feelings about Dr Sam Ryker were strangely confused and, more to the point, unprofessional, and she found the thought oddly troubling. It was probably just as well he was married, she decided. She had come out to Ethiopia to make a fresh start. The last thing she needed was a whole new set of complications in her life.

CHAPTER THREE

'Go away!' Georgia groaned. 'I need my sleep.' She tugged rebelliously at the sheet and was met with firm resistance.

'Come on, sleepyhead.' Jan's voice gradually penetrated the muzziness that seemed to be filling her head. 'I've brought you a cup of coffee. It's strong and black. It'll help you to wake up.'

'I don't want to wake up. My head's only just touched the pillow.'

'I hate to tell you this, but that was twelve hours ago.' This time the sheet was removed forcibly and the smell of coffee wafted under her nose.

Georgia jerked herself from her half-drugged stupor. Groaning into her pillow, she opened one eye to stare furiously at the clock and in a panic sat up, leaping out of bed. Ten o'clock! Oh, no! I should have been up hours ago.'

'Take it easy.' Grinning, Jan pressed the cup of coffee into her hands. 'I decided to let you sleep in. No one expected you to put in an appearance until later anyway.'

Georgia gulped at the coffee as she grabbed her cotton robe. 'I suppose everyone else has been up and working since the crack of dawn.'

'Only those on duty. Look, why don't you get some breakfast then come over to the clinic? Talking of which, I'd better get back. Take your time—I meant it, there's no panic. I'll see you later.' Then with a wave she was gone.

Georgia sat for a few seconds, finishing her coffee, trying to clear her head, then she made a dash for the shower. Fifteen minutes later, slipping on a white coat over a cotton skirt and T-shirt, she decided to skip breakfast and made her way towards the hospital.

Outside a line of patients had already gathered, some squatting, others sitting or standing in a roughly formed queue. They glanced curiously at her, the young women giggling behind their hands, tugging their *shammas* over their heads, though they seemed impervious to the heat which was already creating a steady trickle of sweat between her own shoulder-blades.

A young boy—Georgia guessed he couldn't be more than about eight years old—supported an older man. An infant lay in its mother's arms, wailing softly as she sat, patiently fanning away the flies.

Smiling, Georgia moved to the awning beneath which a table had been set up. One of the young Ethiopian nurses was demonstrating the mixing of baby milk formula and distributing tins of the powder to a small group of obviously new mothers.

Jan greeted her arrival with a grin and beckoned Georgia over. 'Hi, I told you not to hurry.'

'If you hadn't woken me I'd probably have slept for another twelve hours,' Georgia grinned, shamefaced. 'I must have gone out like a light.'

'Forget it,' Jan said.' If it's any consolation we've all been through it. It's a combination of jet-lag and the change of temperature and probably nervous tension. Anyway, come and meet the gang.' She introduced the Ethiopian girl who was similarly swathed in a large plastic apron. 'This is Ofeiba. Ofeiba, this is Dr Maxwell, who's come to help out. There we go. Oh, charming.' She lifted a protesting baby from the scales and held him at arm's length as a steady stream of urine narrowly missed her shoes. 'Well done, young man. There's obviously nothing wrong with your kidneys.' She handed him over to his mother. 'He's doing very nicely and because he had the injections he won't catch measles.'

She waited as Ofeiba translated, then patted the woman's hand, smiling. 'You were very sensible. Your son is strong and healthy. If only we could say the same to them all,' she added less happily as the woman made her way out.

'How's the epidemic?' Georgia queried, glancing through the pile of notes.

'Judging from the number of measles cases we've seen already today, I'd say it's getting worse.' Drying her hands, Jan left Ofeiba to finish handing out the baby food, explaining, 'It acts as an incentive to the mothers to have their babies vaccinated, in those cases where it isn't already too late, of course. Have you seen Sam yet?'

'No. I wasn't sure where he'd be, or where I should start, come to that.'

'Oh, Sam will be doing the ward round. I usually help out when we have our mother-and-baby clinic, which tends to be my responsibility, that and family planning. Ofeiba translates for me, thank heaven,' she laughed. 'Explaining the intricacies of the female reproductive system might be just a little beyond me otherwise.'

'I can imagine.'

'Look, I'm just finishing here. I was going over to the wards anyway, so we may as well go together.'

'How many wards do you have?' Georgia asked, matching her stride to the other girl's as they walked up the incline between the trees.

'Basically three.' Jan pointed to the nearest bungalow. 'That's the women's ward. Over there is the children's ward, but you'll find it tends to cater for mums, sisters and anyone else who accompanies the patient. And this——' she led the way up the steps '—is the men's ward. Come on, I'll show you the layout. We're actually quite well organised.'

Inside, the wooden hospital was one simple long construction, divided into a ward and a small nursing station by a simple screen.

Already the day's heat was beginning to make itself felt and a couple of generator-run fans were whirring, bringing slight relief to some of the obviously more seriously ill patients who were stirring restlessly.

Running a hand across her own forehead, Georgia made her way between the rows of metal-framed beds and found her spirits sinking slightly as her professional gaze swiftly assessed the facilities. She found herself fighting a sense of frustration. For all that the floors were scrubbed and spotlessly clean, and bedspreads and curtains added a brilliant splash of colour, still, she realised, the conditions in which these people worked were primitive compared to those she had enjoyed and even taken for granted back home.

Nothing of her feelings was evident, however, as she made her way along the ward, easing her T-shirt, which was already sticking to her beneath the open white coat, away from her skin.

'I can't promise it will get any better,' Jan smiled sympathetically, 'but you'll get used to it eventually.'

'I hope you're right, or I may not last the month.' She was laughing as Jan held aside the blue curtain drawn around one of the beds.

Sam's gaze rose from the patient he was examining to level with hers. His mouth twisted in faintly sardonic amusement. 'Dr Maxwell, how nice of you to join us. Perhaps now that you're here you'd care to take a look at this patient and give me your opinion?'

Georgia's smile faded and she felt herself flush at the vein of sarcasm in his voice. 'I'm sorry, I overslept. It won't happen again.'

'Forget it.' His blue eyes narrowed briefly, taking in the white coat before he turned his attention back to the man he had been examining. 'This patient has just been admitted. He was seen earlier by Dave at the clinic and referred for immediate admission. Perhaps you'd care to examine him yourself and offer a conclusion as to diagnosis and possible treatment?'

He stood aside and she moved closer. In the process his hand brushed against her arm. Controlling herself with an effort, she briefly scanned the notes he handed over, caught completely off guard by the way her pulse raced, totally illogically, at the brief contact.

It was impossible to distance herself physically from him in the confined space so she did the next best thing, doing so mentally in a cloak of professionalism.

The man could have been aged anything between twenty-five and fifty. He lay on the bed with his eyes closed. He was sweating profusely and he was thin, almost to the point of emaciation.

Georgia felt instinctively for his pulse. It was rapid and his skin felt dry. Taking her stethoscope from her pocket, she smiled at the young nursing assistant who helped the man to sit up and then made a gentle but thorough examination of his chest.

Frowning, she looked up and met Sam's gaze. 'There are coarse crepitations, dry, rubbing sounds, situated posteriorly.'

He nodded, saying nothing.

She settled the man back against the pillows and percussed his chest, tapping two fingers against her hand. 'There's a dull spot here; the resonance is different, flatter.'

Again he said nothing and she found herself stifling a tiny feeling of resentment at being made to feel like a raw medical student all over again. 'He has a cough.' It was a statement, not a question. 'Do we know how long a duration?'

Sam frowned. 'Having spoken to his son, I think we can safely assume it's long-standing. Months rather than weeks.'

'X-rays?'

Sifting through a collection of notes, he handed her a large envelope from which she extracted the film, moving to slot it on to the screen. What she saw made her heart sink. 'What about a sputum check?'

'The results just came through. It's not looking good.' Sam handed her a paper.

Georgia scanned the notes, unconsciously brushing a strand of hair from her eyes as she straightened up and looked at him. 'I'd say we're talking about a case of full-blown tuberculosis here.'

'Right.'

The single word sent a surprising tingle of relief and satisfaction running through her. 'So what can we do?'

His eyes narrowed with frustration. 'Not a lot. If we'd seen him sooner. . . In any reasonably well-equipped hospital I wouldn't have any reservations about the prognosis. Out here. . .' He spread his hands in a gesture of impotence. 'These days, with effective chemotherapy, the mortality-rate from pulmonary tuberculosis is practically nil.'

'Provided the bacilli are not drug-resistant.'

'Well done.'

For some ridiculous reason, the quietly spoken words seemed to bring her confidence flowing back, and, along with it, a tiny spark of resentment. 'You mean I've passed the test? I take it that is what all this was about? A test of my competence.'

His mouth twisted. 'If I'd had any doubts about your competence, believe me, I'd have personally carried you, kicking and screaming if necessary, all the way to Addis and dumped you on the first available flight.'

She stiffened, half stepping back as her gaze shot upwards into the dark eyes which regarded her with a hint of mocking laughter.

'You should come down off that high horse, Dr Maxwell, before you fall off. I don't suppose it would occur to you in a million years that I might simply be asking for a confirmation of my own diagnosis?'

Georgia stared at him and gave a short laugh. 'You do? I mean. . .'

Blue eyes glinted. 'Out here we often survive on nothing more than common sense and a deep-down gut feeling. You must know that pulmonary tuberculosis can be confused with pneumonia or bronchial carcinoma, or even diabetes mellitus. . . Need I go on?' He looked around him, his mouth tightening. 'Every piece of equipment we have needs replacing. The X-ray machine was someone else's reject, disposed of because it was outdated and inefficient, but we were damn grateful to get it.'

Georgia thought of the faded Victorian splendour of her old teaching hospital, with its ancient out-patients' department, the pre-fabricated units, put up to house some of the smaller clinics, originally intended as a temporary measure, but still in use ten years on. The over-worked, often under-staffed departments. 'It makes me realise how well off we were, how much we took for granted,' she said, frowning. 'It seems so unfair.'

'Unfair!' Frustration burned in the depths of his eyes. 'I wake up every day wondering what happened to the justice in this world when some have so much and others have barely enough to survive.'

'You must believe you can change it or you wouldn't be here?'

A small spark of humour returned. 'On a good day I believe it. On a bad day I just get on with the job and tell myself miracles can happen. I'm still waiting.'

'But you're not tempted simply to pack up and leave?'

He gave a short laugh. 'If I thought some other sucker might take over. . .' he gave a lazy grin and her breath caught in her throat '. . .who knows? I'd probably be out of here like a bat out of hell.'

So why didn't she believe it? Georgia thought, with an effort bringing her thoughts under control as she looked at him. 'Which still leaves us with the problem of what to do in this particular case. It's obvious he needs antibiotics.'

Sam's mouth quirked. 'Virtually every patient we have here needs antibiotics of one sort of another. In this particular case we're talking long-term treatment, six months, and even then there's no guarantee that he won't become drug-resistant or develop side-effects.'

'It has to be worth a try.'

Sam looked at the man, checked his pulse, smiling at him as he drew the sheet up over the emaciated limbs. 'Of course it's worth a try. I'll write him up for rifampicin.'

Georgia frowned. 'That's pretty outdated for the treatment of tuberculosis, isn't it?'

'It may be, but it's all we have,' came the quiet rejoinder, 'and we'd better start praying stocks don't run out or that we get some new supplies soon, because there's precious little else.' He straightened up, drawing aside the curtains and moving towards the next bed, speaking to the Ethiopian nursing orderly. 'Asmil, I think you'd better explain to the patient that the drug we're going to give him will turn his urine red.' He chuckled, a deep, throaty, very nice sound, Georgia thought. 'Not only his urine, but his sweat and his tears—otherwise it might come as something of a shock.'

'I do that,' Asmil grinned. 'You leave to me.'

Jan had just finished tepid-sponging the next patient, a younger man, as they drew aside the curtains. She looked up, handing the basin to one of the nurses as she caught Georgia's eye. 'Hi, that was nicely timed. I was just making the patient feel a little more comfortable but we're all finished now.'

Sam scanned the notes, flipping the pages before handing them to Georgia. 'Has there been any change in his condition?'

'Slight, I'd say.'

Georgia returned the clipboard to its place at

the end of the bed. The man who viewed them listlessly was about forty and painfully thin. For a moment her heart sank. Not another case of tuberculosis? 'Do you mind if I take a look?'

Sam raised one dark eyebrow then stood back. 'Go ahead.'

She stood back as Jan drew back the sheet and lifted the man's shirt to reveal a strange lesion on his skin. Flashing her a look of gratitude, Georgia bent to gaze thoughtfully at the sore which was surrounded by tiny red satellite papules.

Very gently she probed the surrounding inflamed area and frowned. 'Hmm, at first sight it looks rather like some kind of bite.' She glanced up. 'Do we have any case history?'

Sam rejected the notes Jan held out to him. 'Insidious onset, low-grade fever, occasional rapid onset of high, intermittent fever.'

Georgia nodded. Again, gently, she made a brief abdominal examination. Straightening up, she said, 'The spleen is enlarged.'

'We did a leucocyte count.' Sam had moved closer now. The subtle scent of musky aftershave drifted into her nostrils, momentarily distracting her, so that her hand shook as she took the notes.

Frowning, she looked up at him. 'He has a slow and progressive anaemia.' She brushed the back of her hand against her brow, feeling the film of sweat. 'I've seen this condition before—not as advanced, but I'm pretty sure this is leishmaniasis.

It's transmitted by the bite of sandflies. There are several variations of the disease. It can affect the gut or the skin in the form of lesions.'

'Ten out of ten.' Sam smiled and, almost without being aware of it, she heaved a sigh of relief. 'Luckily it's fairly easily treated with antimony-based compounds, though you can get resistant cases. We're using Sodium Stibogluconate, injections of six-hundred milligrams.'

'Is it doing the trick?'

He shrugged. 'It's early days yet, but in this case I think we're winning.'

'Isn't the biggest problem prevention?'

He nodded, holding the curtain aside as she went ahead of him. Somehow, in the process, she stumbled over one of the metal legs of a screen and would have fallen if his hand hadn't shot out to steady her.

For several seconds shock held her rigid in the circle of his arms and she was totally unprepared for the primitive way in which, for those fleeting seconds, her body responded to that contact with his taut, masculine body against her own. The sensation was disturbing, far too disturbing. She stiffened. 'I. . .I'm sorry.'

'Think nothing of it.' His glittering gaze narrowed briefly and she was released to move jerkily away as Jan bustled towards them manoeuvring the medications trolley into position in the centre of the ward. 'I'd better write up that Inframpicin.'

Taking a pen from the pocket of his white coat, Sam made an addition to the notes. 'The sooner he gets started on it the better.'

'Thanks,' Jan smiled. 'Where are you off to now?'

'The kiddy department. I thought I'd better take a look at the latest intake.'

'Better brace yourself, then. They're still coming in.' To Georgia she said, 'See you later. Save me a biscuit or two if you get to the coffee first. It's usually a fight to the death if certain people get there first.'

'Will do.' Georgia grinned, thinking that right now she'd gladly forgo the biscuits and just settle for the coffee.

'Ready, Dr Maxwell?' The blue eyes glinted.

'Absolutely.' She almost added 'sir', then thought better of it as she scurried after the rapidly retreating figure.

She caught up with him as he strode up the incline between the trees and it was galling to discover that he wasn't even breathing hard. Either he was superhuman or she was out of condition.

'So, how do you feel about children?'

Her footsteps faltered. 'Children?'

'Yes, you know, those little things. . .'

'I know what children are.' She drew level, breathing hard. 'I simply don't see the relevance. . .'

'How much experience do you have?'

The sardonic gleam wasn't lost on Georgia. She shot him a look. 'On a personal level, very little. If you mean professionally, I enjoyed my stint in paediatrics. . .'

'Good.' He took the bungalow steps two at a time, holding the swing door open as she ducked under his arm. 'Because this is one area where we're always under-staffed. I'm hoping you'll be able to take some of the strain when I'm committed elsewhere.'

She felt a tiny *frisson* of pleasure run through her. 'Just tell me where to start.' She was heading for the ward when his hand caught her arm and he swung her to face him. She was conscious of a whole vortex of emotions that surged over her, leaving her feeling ridiculously breathless as she looked into his eyes.

'A word of warning. Don't equate this with anything you've come across back home, because you'll be in for a shock.'

The intensity in his voice shook her and she frowned uncertainly. 'I can handle it.'

'I hope so,' his voice hardened, 'because life expectancy out here, especially of children, is short. Any child who makes it to the age of four is lucky, though I use the term advisedly.'

Georgia drew a breath and nodded. 'Thanks for reminding me.'

He looked at her for a second then said, 'Come

and meet Sister Abuna.' He led the way to where a group of young, dark-skinned girls in loosely fitting dresses and white aprons were grouped around a slightly older woman. She was bathing an infant who couldn't have been more than a few hours old.

She looked up, beaming, as they approached. 'Dr Sam.'

He smiled. 'Sister, I'd like you to meet our latest recruit. This is Dr Maxwell, Georgia Maxwell, from England.'

'Dr Maxwell.'

'Georgia, please.'

'Sister Abuna is in charge of this ward. She trained in Addis and came to us about twelve months ago.' He grinned. 'We're lucky to have her, as she so often reminds us. She also runs our mother-and-baby classes.'

Looking at the group of girls, Georgia guessed that the oldest couldn't have been more than fifteen. 'So, how's this little chap, then?'

'He's doing fine.' Laughing, Sister Abuna ran a hand over the naked body, dispersing the water before wrapping the squalling infant firmly in a towel. 'He doesn't like the bath too much.'

'No, I don't imagine he does. Let's take a quick look at him while we're here, shall we?' Sam took the baby and spoke to the girl who reached out, smiling, to run a finger against the baby's soft, downy cheek. 'This is the baby's mother. Her name is Bizunesh.' He spoke to her in her own language and she responded, smiling shyly at Georgia.

'What did she say?'

'She says you are very welcome.'

Georgia acknowledged the greeting with a smile and a nod. 'She's beautiful, isn't she? How old is she and is this her first child?'

Checking the baby's hips, Sam spoke again to the girl. 'Bizunesh is fifteen and this is her third child. The first died at birth, the second lived for three days.' He looked at Georgia. 'Luckily she heard about our hospital and this time, when she knew her time was close, she walked for five days to get to us.'

'Five days!'

'That's not unusual.' Sam glanced up before his hands moved with surprising gentleness over the tiny, wriggling form, testing its reflexes as he held its hands, lifting it to see how it supported its head, running a fingertip against the base of its foot, again watching as the toes curled under. 'Well, that all looks nice and healthy.'

Grinning, he handed the infant back to its mother where it nuzzled against her breasts, the tiny mouth puckering as it scented milk. 'At least this one looks as if it's going to make it. Come on.' His hand was on Georgia's arm. 'I'll show you the rest of the ward.'

He was right, Georgia realised as they made a

steady progress from bed to bed. It was unlike anything she had ever experienced back in England. The first thing she noticed here was the comparative silence. The children, aged anything from a few days to about ten years, lay in cots or beds with safety-rails. For the most part they slept or stared listlessly at what was going on around them. Some whimpered, some tossed restlessly, runny-nosed, red-eyed, pitifully thin.

Sam paused to brush a hand over one small, sweating brow and to speak reassuringly to the woman seated beside the bed. 'These are the latest arrivals. This one was admitted this morning, presenting with a high fever. Do you want to take a look?'

'Do you mind?'

'Go ahead.'

'Does she have a cough?' The child, about four years old, lay unmoving as Georgia checked her pulse. Sister Abuna came to stand at the foot of the bed.

'Yes, the mother says it started about four days ago.'

Georgia nodded. 'There's some swelling of the eyelids and photophobia—light-sensitivity.' Uncoiling her stethoscope, she listened to the small chest, then she checked inside the child's mouth, the presence of tiny, white Koplik's spots on the mucous membrane confirming her suspicions. 'I'm afraid you've got another case of measles on your hands and, if I'm not very much mistaken, there's a secondary infection bubbling away in there.'

Sam nodded. 'That's pretty much what I was afraid of. Pneumonia is nearly always an added complication in these children. They come to us in such a malnourished state, they have no natural resistance to infection.' He dragged a hand wearily through his hair, leaving a tuft standing on end.

For some reason it made him seem oddly vulnerable and Georgia found herself having to resist an urge to reach out and smooth it down. She said wryly, 'Isolation is hardly an option, is it? How about antibiotics?'

'That at least we can do.' He wrote up the notes, handing them to Sister Abuna. 'Keep an eye on her. Let me know if there's any marked deterioration and I'll be straight over.'

They left her gently rearranging the sheet as they moved towards the next bed.

'What happens to the patients you can't find beds for?' Georgia found herself automatically examining a badly infected wound as Sam checked a drip on an infant in one of the nearby cots.

He glanced over his shoulder at her. 'We manage somehow or other. We have several small hostels, dotted around the grounds. Relatives bring their own food and cooking-pots. It helps to keep costs low. Ideally we try to be self-sufficient. It doesn't always work, in which case if supplies don't get through, or the rains don't come, then I'm afraid we all have to tighten our belts.'

Georgia straightened, easing her back after applying a sachet of antiseptic solution to the open wound. Sam turned the tiny infant with a gentleness that fascinated her before he looked up. 'Finished?'

She nodded and they made a steady progress along the ward. Georgia smiled at a boy of about eight holding a younger child, little more than a baby. Her head rested against his shoulder and her large brown eyes were expressionless as she wailed softly.

Sam paused to put an arm round the boy's shoulders. 'This is Abraha. He and his sister came to us three days ago.'

Georgia smiled. 'Hello, Abraha.'

The boy drew a blanket protectively over his sister. 'Where are their parents?'

Murmuring something softly and ruffling the boy's hair, Sam moved on, but not before she had seen the fleeting tautness of his features. 'Their mother died on the journey, about two weeks ago.'

Georgia stared at him. 'Died? Two weeks? But. . .'

'Abraha carried his sister through the mountain pass. He couldn't do anything for his mother. He had nothing left in his village to return to. His father died of tuberculosis as far as we can make out.'

She swallowed hard. 'So what will happen to them now?'

'They'll stay here. At least they won't starve. They may even get a little education. They'll be safe.'

Georgia drew a breath, fighting a sudden, almost overwhelming sense of desolation. She brought it quickly under control. He was right—this was a different world. She had known it would be, but nothing, no amount of reading, could possibly have prepared her for the reality of the conditions in which these people lived, the suffering they endured so uncomplainingly. More amazing, perhaps, was their apparently stoical acceptance. It was almost as if life was cheap, expendable, yet, looking at their faces, she knew it wasn't true.

Her feelings were more or less under control as she exchanged a smiling greeting with the girl who sat rocking a baby in her arms. A nursing orderly, wearing a scarf over her hair and an apron over her brightly coloured dress, approached with a bottle of milk formula, helping the mother to guide the baby's tiny, button mouth on to the teat. It lay listlessly, unmoving, although, Georgia guessed, it must be hungry.

'How long has she been here?' She was

aware of Sam reaching for the notes.

'She came today.' The orderly folded a towel and gathered up baby lotion and power.

Georgia ran a finger over the baby's skin. It felt dry and had an almost translucent look about it, confirming her suspicion that it was badly dehydrated. 'Will you ask her how old her baby is?'

Smiling, the orderly said something in her own language. The girl's answer was little more than a shy whisper.

'She says three months.'

Georgia swallowed hard. 'Surely there must be some mistake. Does she mean three weeks?' She looked at Sam. Or even three days, the thought ran through her mind.

He held out the notes, watching as she stared at them. 'Her milk dried up,' he said evenly. 'Her village is remote, over the mountains. They had no supplies, no milk formula.'

'You're saying the baby has had no food for. . . for days, maybe longer?' Her mouth felt dry, then, even as some kind of protest rose to her lips, almost without her being aware of it, she was aware of Sam's hand under her arm, leading her away.

They emerged into the raw afternoon heat. She broke away from him to stand, gripping the veranda rail, breathing hard.

'Are you all right?'

She brushed a strand of hair from her eyes as

she straightened up, turning to look at him. In a lowered tone she said, 'How old is she?'

His gaze levelled with hers. 'Thirteen.'

She nodded, trying to dislodge the tight knot of anger that was suddenly filling her throat. 'I see. And where is her husband?'

Sam quirked an eyebrow. 'She has no husband.'

She pressed the back of her hand against her mouth. 'Someone is responsible.'

His mouth tightened. 'I warned you against applying western standards. It doesn't work that way out here.'

'So you're saying that that girl. . .she's scarcely more than a child herself. . .is to blame?' she challenged.

His gaze narrowed. '*I'm* not the one apportioning blame.'

'How very convenient, and how like a man.' She had half turned away in disgust but, suddenly, his hand closed over her arm, whirling her round to face him.

'You know you're being unreasonable.'

'I *feel* unreasonable.' Two spots of angry colour flared in her cheeks as she faced him. 'I feel *damned* unreasonable.'

'We'd all like to live in a perfect world but it's never going to be that way. The sooner you get used to the idea the better.' Georgia tried to wrench herself free but his grip merely tightened. 'She has no husband in the true sense, or the sense as you recognise it. She is a temporary wife.'

'Temporary. . .?' She gave a short laugh.

'It isn't unusual out here. Montagwach took her to live with him and if she bears him a healthy, living child. . .'

'Don't tell me, let me guess. He may do her the honour of marrying her?'

'I may not like it,' Sam said evenly, 'but nothing I can do is going to change things, at least not overnight. You may find the idea of child marriages repellent. These people don't see it that way. Most girls consider it an honour to be chosen.'

She stared at him. 'So you're saying I should ignore it?'

'If you want to stay out here and still retain some degree of sanity, then yes, that's what I'm saying.'

She flexed her imprisoned hand. Frustratingly his grip tightened again, sending a tingling awareness of him surging through her. She resisted it. 'And so it goes on,' she bit out. 'You've seen those children, those babies. They're all as close to starvation as it's possible to come and still live. Do any of the emergency relief supplies get through?'

'Not enough. There's a system but it's only as good as the strongest link.' His mouth twisted. 'I worked for six months in an area where conditions were pretty much like these. And yes, they got deliveries of American grain. The system for distributing it was that each family got a measure of grain depending on the weight of the smallest child in each family. You want to know what happened, Dr Maxwell?' He jerked her roughly towards him when she would have turned away. 'Well, I'll tell you. One child, probably the smallest and weakest anyway, was starved, yes, starved, while the rest of the family ate, so that when the grain arrived the man distributing it would weigh the smallest child to assess the needs of the family, and that family would then be given a more generous ration. I don't like it either but it happens and I can't change it, even though my blood boils at the bloody unfairness of it.'

She swallowed hard and said gruffly, 'You're doing the best you can and it does make a difference. I'm sorry, I shouldn't have said what I did. Some of those children are alive who wouldn't otherwise be. No one expects miracles.'

His mouth twisted. 'I'd like to believe that's true. I wonder if you have any idea just what you're getting yourself into?'

His sudden, slow smile did things to her already over-worked pulse-rate. They stared into each other's eyes and he raised his hand slowly to trace the line of her cheek, drawing her towards him. For an instant she resisted, then his lips brushed against hers, softly, unhurriedly, before he tensed, then she was free.

'I'll see you in the morning,' he said softly.

She nodded, confusion clouding her eyes as she acknowledged an inner sense of disappointment. What *was* she getting herself into? The thought stayed with her as, much later, she showered and climbed, exhausted, into bed, and was still unresolved as she fell into a restless sleep.

CHAPTER FOUR

IT WAS the coolest part of the day, but, even so, a hot breeze ruffled the few trees next morning as Georgia made her way to the hospital.

Smiling a greeting at the group of women who sat with their babies in one of the few patches of shade that would disappear as the sun rose higher, she ran lightly up the steps and, shrugging herself into her white coat, made her way to the small surgery.

A fan whirred noisily, redistributing heat rather than giving out any real physical relief, and she noticed several of the post-operative patients stirring restlessly.

Jan greeted her arrival with a smile as Georgia walked into the small department. 'Hi, sleep well?'

'Like a log,' Georgia grinned. Determined not to be late, she had purposely set her alarm half an hour earlier than was strictly necessary. 'Exhaustion helps. What have we got today, then?' She peered at the list Jan handed to her. 'Hmm, it looks as if we're in for a pretty busy morning. I think we'd better make a start.'

'It gets worse.' Jan's face dimpled. 'That's just for starters.'

'You're great for my morale, you know that?' Taking a deep breath, Georgia nodded. 'Right, let's go.'

Seating herself at the well-worn table, she stifled a tiny feeling of depression as she quickly studied the tray of very basic drugs and treatments which were available to her.

More than once during that morning, as she worked her way through the steady procession of patients, she felt an enormous sense of gratitude to Jan and to Dena Kindwe, the little Ethiopian nursing orderly who also acted as interpreter.

Georgia wiped a droplet of sweat from her eyes, feeling dust and perspiration on her skin and lips as she finished dressing a particularly nasty leg ulcer. The man lying on the examination couch was thirty, but looked sixty. As Jan passed another melonil dressing, Georgia felt her throat tighten as he lay, expressionless, despite the pain he must be feeling, even though she was doing her best to minimise it.

Easing her back, she managed, with an effort, to force a smile. 'Tell him the dressings should help the ulcer to heal, but he must try to keep it dry.'

Fat chance of that, she thought as she waited for the girl to interpret. When the only source of water was a disease-infested river used for bathing, drinking and, often, by animals, the odds were already too heavily stacked against the most basic of hygienic standards. 'Tell him he must boil the water before he uses it.' She counted out a supply of tablets, dropping them into a container and sealing it. 'These will help his leg to heal. He must take three every day until they are finished.'

The man nodded as he was helped, gently, from the couch to shuffle his way out.

'Why do I get the feeling I'm fighting a losing battle?' Georgia scrubbed her hands in an earthenware basin, straightening her shoulders wearily for a moment.

'You just have to keep hoping the message will eventually get through.' Jan looked at her with a slight smile.

'I've always thought of myself as an optimist. I'm not so sure any more.' Georgia gave a wry smile. 'Let's have the next one, shall we?'

The next patient, an elderly woman, was helped into the room by a young girl. She was limping, her bare feet were badly swollen, and the skin on one foot was dry and scaly and dotted with lesions.

It was only as she knelt to make her examination that Georgia realised that one toe was actually missing, and several of the others were already deformed and badly infected.

She drew a breath, looking up at the girl. 'How long has she been like this?'

Dena interpreted. The younger girl replied.

'She says maybe a long time, slowly, so that they not notice until her mother was not able to walk without falling.'

Georgia bit at her lower lip as she ran a finger over the area of inflamed skin, watching the woman's face carefully for a reaction as she did so. Even the fairly firm pressure she exerted seemed to bring no response.

Straightening, she met Jan's look. 'I'd say there's almost total sensory loss.' Frowning, she bent to study the affected limb again, looking more closely this time at the raised, hypopigmented lesions. Turning to Jan, she said softly, 'You must have seen more cases like this than I have.' She straightened up. 'I'd say this is an advanced case of leprosy. What do you think?'

Jan questioned the woman, listening carefully to her stumbling replies before looking at Georgia. 'I haven't actually seen too many cases, surprisingly enough, but I think you're right. It's an almost classic presentation.'

Georgia nodded. 'It's the sensory loss that causes the secondary damage. This whole area here is affected, which means that she isn't aware of any injury or damage to the foot. Look.' She pointed out a paler area. 'That was probably a burn. She wouldn't have felt it, but it took off a layer of skin, leaving it open to infection. That's probably how she lost the toe.'

'But we can treat it?'

Georgia nodded. 'The problem is, it requires long-term medication and some patients develop a resistance to the drugs.' She frowned. 'I can start her off on a course of Rifampicin which should make her non-infectious. She'll need a course of Dapsone as well; hopefully it should prevent her resistance. We may have to change to Clofazimine, but let's see how we go. Is she going to be able to attend the clinic on a fairly regular basis?'

Dena spoke to the younger girl, who nodded. 'She says she will come with her mother.'

'Fine,' Georgia smiled. 'The other thing is to try and teach her how to cope with that numbed foot. She has to learn how to make allowances, to prevent any more damage. That way we can prevent any new infections, though I wouldn't count on it.'

Jan, dispensing the medication, was more philosophical. 'Have a little faith. At least we can do something. A few years ago there wouldn't have been any treatment. In most leprosy cases, people simply became more and more disfigured and helpless, until they became outcasts. This must be progress of a kind.'

For the rest of the morning they worked solidly. By midday the sun was directly overhead, the air stifling, taking Georgia's breath away. Using her forearm to wipe away the film of sweat, she eased the white coat from her clammy skin. 'Any more patients, or have we finished?'

'Just one.' Jan dropped the used instruments into the steriliser. 'She arrived about half an hour ago. She seems quite distressed. I thought you'd want to see her.'

'Yes, of course.' Georgia was already heading for the door. 'Do we know anything about her?'

'Dena's with her now. She's trying to get as much information as possible. It's not always easy with the young girls. They're naturally shy, often little more than children. I thought it might be best to let her speak to someone in her own language.'

'You did the right thing.' Georgia pushed open the surgery door. The girl was sitting on the bed, her head and shoulders covered by her *shamma*. Dena was holding her hand, speaking softly to her.

Georgia smiled. 'Will you explain to her that I am a doctor, that she mustn't be afraid? I am going to try to help her.'

Dena translated. The girl smiled, responding shyly. 'She is very grateful.'

Georgia moved closer. 'Can she tell us about herself and her problem?'

Dena spoke to the girl again before turning to Georgia. 'She says her name is Yahasba. She comes from a small village a long way from here. She has walked for twelve days to get to the hospital.'

Georgia drew in a breath, telling herself that for the sake of her own sanity she had to learn to accept what, out here, was the norm. But it wasn't going to be easy. 'How old is she?'

'She says sixteen.'

With an effort, Georgia forced a smile as she took the girl's hand, murmuring the few words of comfort and welcome she had managed to pick up since her arrival. The girl's brown eyes stared at her, holding a mixture of fear and confusion.

'Tell her not to be afraid. We're here to help. Ask if she can explain what is wrong with her.'

'I think I may be able to save you the trouble, if it will help?' Sam spoke from the doorway.

Georgia's glance flickered over his fawn trousers, the pale blue shirt, unbuttoned at the neck, exposing the bronzed column of his throat. Warm colour suffused her cheeks as she closed her eyes for a brief moment, shutting out the image. He was far too attractive for her peace of mind.

'I thought you were in theatre.' She swallowed hard. 'I'd appreciate it, if you have the time.'

'It's no problem. Do you mind if I take a look?'

His own gaze lingered on the white cotton trousers she had elected to wear. They might not be fashionable, but at least they offered some protection to her legs from the seemingly endless army of marauding flies and insects. She had chosen the baggy, coral-coloured shirt for the same reason. Its turn-back sleeves left her arms exposed, but her neck and shoulders protected.

What a sight she must look. Restively, she tucked a stray tendril of hair behind her ear.

'No, of course not; I'd be grateful.' She moved aside. He leaned forward, speaking gently to the girl, carrying out his own brief examination before turning to Georgia again.

'As I suspected, she has a small fistula, a hole in her bladder.'

'I know what a fistula is,' she frowned. 'What I don't understand is why. It isn't something you'd normally associate with someone of this age.'

'Unfortunately we see too many cases like this out here.' Sam's mouth was a taut line of weariness as he drew her away. 'They all have one thing in common when they arrive here. They all feel dirty and ashamed.'

'I'm not sure I understand what you're saying. Why should they feel ashamed?'

'Because their families don't want them; it's as simple as that.' He pushed open the swing door and she stepped out into the glaring brilliance. 'That child was in labour for five days, struggling to give birth to a baby that was too big and lying awkwardly. Can you imagine what that must have been like? Without drugs to ease the pain, with no one to help. She was lucky,' he said tersely, 'she survived.'

Georgia shot him a quick look. 'What happened to the baby?'

'It was alive when she last saw it, but in the

process of giving birth her bladder was torn. The result is that every time she stands up she pours a trickle of urine on to the floor. It's constant and there's nothing she can do about it.'

Georgia looked at him. 'And how old is the baby?'

'About six months.'

'Oh, no!' Georgia felt her heart go out to the young girl. 'And she's been like this ever since?'

He nodded grimly. 'She stayed in bed for a couple of weeks, thinking it might make things better, but then her husband insisted she must look after the baby and make his food. When she got up, nothing had changed. Urine was still trickling down her legs, soaking her clothes.'

Georgia straightened her shoulders and looked at him. In a lowered tone she said, 'What happened?'

His blue eyes narrowed with frustration. 'What always happens. Her husband and her mother-in-law finally couldn't tolerate it any longer. They refused to live with the smell and she was driven out.'

'And. . .what happened to the baby?'

'She left it behind. There was no way she could feed it, care for it.' Sam's mouth twisted. 'I'd say its chances of survival were probably minimal anyway. From what she says, the labour was traumatic. It was probably starved of oxygen. Chances are it's already dead.'

'So. . .she just started walking? Alone?'

'The general hospitals won't take these cases. There are too many.' His mouth twisted. 'They don't want their beds and sheets soaked with urine; it isn't hygienic.'

'So she came here.'

'There's nowhere else for them to go. Word gets around. We never turn them away, they know that.'

She walked beside him, matching her stride to his. 'At least the treatment is relatively straight-forward, a fairly minor surgical procedure.'

'It shouldn't be necessary.' His mouth tightened. 'It wouldn't be necessary, if we could only change attitudes.'

'I thought you said we shouldn't judge by western standards?' She looked up to see him regarding her with cynical amusement.

'I'm not immune to some good old-fashioned frustration every now and again.'

'It isn't going to happen overnight.'

'I don't imagine it will.' His gaze shifted slowly over her slender shape, taking in the curve of her hips and the line of her legs. She was suddenly, tautly conscious of him.

'So, what will you do?'

'Do?' He shrugged. 'I suppose I shall keep on keeping on, as they say. What else is there? If we fail them, who else is there?'

Her brow furrowed. 'There must be times when

you feel you're fighting a losing battle.'

'If I really thought that, I wouldn't be here. I suppose there's also a certain stubbornness factor.' His gaze levelled with hers. 'Once I've made up my mind to do something I seldom change it.'

For a long moment she held her breath as Sam's eyes looked directly into hers, then, with a jerky movement, she turned away, relieved to have her attention caught by the small group of women gathered round a small fire in one of the clearings.

A smell of cooking drifted into her nostrils, making her feel oddly light-headed, and she remembered that, in her determination not to be late, she had skipped breakfast.

'What are they cooking?'

'It's called *injara*. It's a kind of bread.'

She looked at him, wrinkling her nose. 'You mean that flat, rubbery-looking grey stuff? It's the funniest-looking bread I've ever seen.'

He laughed. 'It's made from *teff*, a cereal grain. The texture is a bit gritty and it has a slightly bitter taste, but you soon get used to it.'

She shuddered slightly. 'Thanks, I think I'll take your word for it. What about the stuff in the pot?'

He smiled slightly, amused by her curiosity. 'That is *wat*, a stew made of meat or chicken. It's probably a bit too highly spiced for your uninitiated taste buds.'

'It smells good.'

'It *is* good. You should try it some time.'

'Maybe I will, though right now I'd gladly settle for a cup of coffee.' She turned, smiling, and was totally unprepared for the sudden wave of dizziness that hit her, or the wave of lethargy that seemed to be sweeping over her. Maybe skipping breakfast hadn't been such a good idea after all. Almost without being aware of it, she brushed a hand weakly across her forehead.

He was instantly concerned. 'Are you all right?'

'What?' She moistened her dry lips. 'Yes. . .I'm fine, just a little dizzy for a few seconds, that's all. It. . .must be the heat.' At least she told herself it was the heat. His nearness was oddly unnerving.

'You could do with a break, some shade.'

She shook her head and immediately wished she hadn't as her head began to throb. 'I'll be fine, really. I still have to finish. . .'

'That can wait.' His mouth tightened. 'Surely you of all people must know the importance of keeping up your fluid levels in this heat—and when did you last eat?'

'I don't remember,' she muttered defensively.

He swore softly. 'What did you have for breakfast?'

'I don't usually bother. . .'

His mouth took on an ominously angry look. 'You crazy little fool. Don't you know better than to let yourself become dehydrated?'

'I have patients waiting.' She tossed her head back with restless frustration and Sam studied her in silence, taking in the firm set of her mouth, the truculence in the taut angle of her jaw.

'There'll always be patients waiting,' he ground out.

'I don't need you to tell me how to do my job,' she breathed raggedly, the curve of her breasts slowly rising with the motion. 'I'm perfectly capable of deciding what is in my own best interest.' She swallowed hard, feeling strangely at odds with herself. What was it about this man that seemed to have such an unsettling effect on her? Her voice wavered. 'I'll take a break as soon as I've finished.'

She made to turn away but he stopped her, his hands closing on her shoulders, drawing her around to face him.

'You'll take a break now. What use do you think you'll be to anyone if you can't even stay on your feet?'

'Has anyone ever told you you're a bully, Dr Ryker?' she muttered.

A nerve pulsed in his jaw. 'Frequently.'

She could believe it. He was staring down at her, his eyes glinting, his gaze roaming over her flushed cheeks. She sensed a tautening of his muscles, heard his sharp intake of breath and found herself watching in rapt fascination as his face loomed closer, and his utterly sensuous mouth took possession of her own.

The sensation was electric. Her head went back

as, with a superhuman effort, she raised her eyes to his. Her nostrils were filled with the warm, musky, male scent of him, teasing her senses, filling her with confusion. This shouldn't be happening. She dragged her gaze away and said throatily, 'What exactly is it that you want from me, Sam?'

'Want?' His voice was husky. 'Maybe you shouldn't ask. This is crazy. . .'

She had to agree. She moistened her dry lips with the tip of her tongue. His eyes flared and she held her breath, knowing he was going to kiss her again.

A totally unbidden quiver of desire shuddered through her as the kiss seemed to snatch up the shreds of her resistance, making her suddenly, vitally aware of her body's needs. It was totally unlike anything she had ever experienced before. She gasped at the aggressive thoroughness with which he forced her lips apart as his tongue invaded the softness of her mouth, sending a sensation so exquisite coursing through her that her body betrayed her with its instant response. In all the times Martin had kissed her it had never been like this.

Moaning softly, she swayed towards him and her fingers rose to tangle in the darkness of his hair. For an instant she felt him tense, then he set her free, his breathing harsh as he drew away.

'Hell!'

She stared at him in drugged confusion, then became dizzily aware of the door opening and the figure standing there.

'Sam, thank heavens I found you.' Dave's voice intruded into the tension.

She was vaguely aware, as the warm colour surged into her cheeks, of Sam's blue eyes darkening, then realised he was deliberately shielding her from the other man's view, giving her precious moments to recover her composure.

She could only guess at how she must look. Her mouth felt swollen and her cheeks were flushed.

'There's an urgent radio call from one of the supply depots. It could be trouble.'

'I'll be right there.' Sam was already heading in the direction of the administration block, the incident of only a few moments ago already clearly banished from his mind. As if it had never happened, she thought, her hand going shakily to her lips where she could still feel the pressure of that kiss.

He turned to fling a look in her direction. 'Get some food.'

She nodded without speaking. She felt dazed by her reaction to a man she scarcely knew, bewildered by the welter of sensations she had experienced in his arms. He was right, it was crazy. Sam was a married man and the idea that she was actually jealous hit her like a physical blow.

CHAPTER FIVE

IT WAS galling to discover that he was right, Georgia thought as she dabbed at her mouth. She did feel better for having eaten.

'Anyone for more coffee?' Dave was already helping himself from the Thermos jugs which had been left on a tray.

Georgia drained her cup, handing it over. 'Mm, yes please, it's delicious.'

'It should be.' He refilled her cup. 'Help yourself to sugar. Coffee was first discovered in Ethiopia by a goat herder, about a thousand years ago. They're experts at it.'

'I didn't know that.'

'Not many people do,' he grinned, white teeth emphasised by his deep tan. 'But it's true.'

'Oh, if that's coffee I'll have mine black with three sugars.'

'Heathen!'

'I don't care, I need it.' Jan collapsed, groaning, into a chair, fanning herself with a magazine. 'It's definitely the best offer I've had all day so far.'

Georgia laughed. 'Problems?' She was on her feet, helping herself to sugar.

'You could say. Some of the first batch of

measles cases are starting to get better. It's like bedlam over there. Mind you——' she launched herself to her feet to reach for an apple '—I'd much rather see them like this than the state they were in when they arrived. If I'm honest, I didn't think some of them would make it.'

'That's the miracle of modern medicine for you.' Dave's brow furrowed as he lifted the lid on one of the serving-dishes, leaning forward to sniff at the contents. 'Jeez! What is this stuff?'

Georgia laughed. 'It's actually very nice. It's beef curry.'

He threw her a sceptical look. 'More like goat. Look, I recognise it. That's the one. . .'

She hit out playfully at him. 'Shut up and eat, unless you want to start a mutiny.'

'OK, OK.' He held up his hands in mock-submission.

'Just don't leave it too long before you go for fresh supplies,' Jan interceded, smiling. 'I'd give my eye-teeth for a real omelette, made with speckly brown eggs, filled with mushrooms and cheese. . .'

'Try the goat——' Dave slapped a plate into her hand '—and dream on.'

The playful banter was, Georgia recognised, a kind of escape mechanism, a way of relieving the tension they were all under, had been under for a great deal longer than herself. They ate reasonably well, the Ethiopian cooks making the best use of dried and canned goods which would keep them going until fresh supplies from one of the relief organisations reached them.

The door opened and Oz came in with a tall Ethiopian woman. She was wearing a white coat and she was strikingly beautiful, slim, slender-necked, her hair coiled on top of her head. The kind of looks, Georgia thought, which could have graced any top fashion magazine.

'Georgia,' Oz beamed. 'We seem to keep missing you.'

'Oh, I'm still finding my way around.' She smiled. 'Do you want coffee?'

'Try the goat pie,' Dave quipped.

Oz raised an eyebrow quizzically. 'Goat pie?'

'Ignore him.' Smiling wryly, she poured two cups of coffee, handing them over.

'Ah, yes, the joke.'

'You've been in Theatre all morning?'

'They like to keep us busy, you know.' He glanced at the woman beside him. 'Have you met Dr Moulou?'

'No, I'm afraid I haven't.' Georgia smilingly held out a hand.

'We always seem to be passing in opposite directions. Please call me Ana—everyone does.'

Georgia found herself taking an instant liking to the young woman. 'How long have you been with the team?'

Ana smiled, taking a tray and helping herself

to fresh fruit and coffee. 'At the hospital? About four years. Dr Geoff was here when I arrived. At first my job was to assist and learn so that I could go out to the villages to carry out minor surgery. Later I was able to help here at the hospital.' They joined the others at one of the tables.

Georgia said, 'I gather there are sometimes as many as three operating theatres in use at any one time now.'

'Word soon gets around.' Jan peeled a banana. 'People come here because the hospitals in the city either can't or won't take them and Geoff would never turn anyone away.'

'We have many fistula cases.' Ana looked at Georgia with sombre, dark eyes.

'Yes, I'm ashamed to say I hadn't realised quite how prevalent the condition was until I came out here.'

'It was the reason he first opened the hospital. He saw the need.' Ana raised a slender hand. 'Where else would these poor girls go if we didn't help them?'

'Ana is one of our most competent surgeons,' Dave put in. 'We're lucky to have her.'

'Oh?' Georgia turned to smile enquiringly at the girl. 'Did you do your medical training in Addis Ababa?'

A small ripple of laughter ran through the group and she felt herself flush. What had she said that was so funny?

'Ana has no officially recognised qualification,' Dave said.

Georgia stared at him and shook her head. 'But. . .I don't understand.'

'Ana was a fistula case herself, isn't that right, Ana?'

'It is true.' She smiled. 'I had heard of Dr Geoff and the hospital. I knew it was my only hope, so I came here, walking for many days from my village, and because when I was cured I had nowhere to go I stayed—at first to help, later to learn.' She sipped at her coffee. 'At that time there was only Dr Geoff and one other doctor to deal with so many cases, so I watched, and after a while I was allowed to help nurse the patients and then to assist in Theatre.'

'And when did you start to operate?'

'That was Sam's doing.' Ana's smile faded slightly. 'Dr Geoff was sick, but the fistula cases still came, and Sam refused to turn them away. So I began to operate.' She laughed slightly. 'Don't worry, at first I was supervised, until one day Sam said I was ready to perform surgery alone.'

'And she's been at it ever since. Much to our relief, I might add.' Dave grinned. 'We need all the extra pairs of hands we can get. I've even offered to teach her how to fly the plane.'

Georgia joined in the laughter, which was shattered by the sharp opening of the door. Sam came into the room, his face taut. 'We've had an emergency call.'

'Hell, no. Where from?' Dave was instantly on his feet, swiftly followed by the rest.

'Dashan.'

'Jeez, no.' Dave brushed a hand through his hair.

'What's happened?' Georgia looked quickly at Sam.

He said grimly, 'Dashan is a resource depot, a dumping ground, if you like, for the relief agencies who fly in blankets, food and drugs. They also run a small clinic. They're dotted around, on the principle that, out here, you never put all your eggs in one basket.' He raked a hand through his hair. 'Every now and again rebels cross the border, usually from Somalia, and help themselves to our supplies. They must have known a new load had recently been flown in and was awaiting distribution.'

'How bad is it?' Dave said grimly.

'Bad enough. A couple of aid workers and several of the locals have been hurt. One is dead. As far as I can gather, some of the others have gunshot wounds. We won't have the full picture until we get out there. We'll take the truck. Oz, you can come with me.'

Georgia was already heading for the door. 'You're going to need all the help you can get. Just give me five minutes to get my things. . .'

'Don't bother. You won't be going.'

She stared at him. 'But. . .'

His face was drawn into a frown. 'You'd only be in the way. Besides, you'll be more useful here.'

'I see.' The words came out thickly as she shied away from the impatience in his gaze, but he was already striding away and, illogically, tears swam into her eyes. So, in spite of everything, he still thought of her as a liability. She blinked rapidly. Clearly nothing had changed.

She was vaguely aware of the others drifting away and thought she was alone until Dave spoke.

'Don't take it personally. He doesn't mean anything by it, you know.'

Georgia drew a deep breath. 'I'm sorry?'

'It's just Sam being Sam. That's the way he is.'

'Mean and moody, you mean?'

He laughed. 'I guess it can seem that way, until you get to know him.'

But wasn't that precisely what she thought she had been doing? she thought, stifling a sigh. It only went to prove how wrong you could be. With an effort she summoned a smile. 'I'll take your word for it. It's just that I somehow get the distinct impression that I'm on trial here, and I'm not sure what I have to do to prove myself.'

'Hey, Sam probably thinks you need time to adjust, that's all. It can take a while to get acclimatised. Heat can play some pretty funny tricks with the system.'

Couldn't it just? Wryly, she said, 'Do you always spring so readily to his defence?'

He gave a boyish grin. 'Not when he's around. I value my life.'

In spite of herself, Georgia threw back her head and laughed, then she said more soberly, 'You've known him for some time?'

He shrugged. 'We go back a long way. Sam was in the States for a while. We met when he was doing a series of lectures. After that we sort of went our separate ways for a year or so. We managed to keep in touch every once in a while. Then I heard, some time later, that Sam was out here. I applied to join the project.' He proffered a glass of fruit juice which she refused, shaking her head.

'You like him, don't you?'

'I respect the man. Ideals are hard come by. With some people they can disappear pretty fast when the going gets rough, but not with Sam. Yeah, I like him.' Dave frowned. 'One way or another he's had a pretty tough time of it, what with Megan and all.'

'Megan?'

'Sure, his wife.'

So that was her name. Georgia felt as if a heavy weight was suddenly pressing down on her shoulders. She swallowed hard. 'I suppose it can't be easy, with Sam working out here and. . .'

Dave shot her a look. 'Sam's being out here

doesn't have anything to do with it. He and Megan parted company before he took on this job.'

Georgia stared at him. 'I'm sorry. I had no idea.'

'There's no reason why you should.'

'Do you. . .know what happened?'

He shook his head. 'I heard she walked out. Sam doesn't talk about it and I don't ask. All I know is that he came out here soon after.' He suddenly looked at his watch. 'Hell, is that the time? I shouldn't be here.'

Georgia fled too, hurrying up the slope between the trees. The heat was, if anything, even more intense now, and she wished, as she ran up the steps, that she had taken time to shower and change instead of having that extra cup of coffee.

Completing her examination of her latest patient, she listened to the short, painful, dry cough of the woman lying on the examination couch, her body shaking with rigor as she clung pathetically to the anxious-looking child who had accompanied her to the clinic.

Careful to avoid any sudden change of facial expression, so as not to alarm the child, Georgia spoke softly to Jan. 'She's coughing up blood. Her respiration is rapid too, forty per minute. How's the temperature?'

Frowning, Jan shook down the thermometer. 'Forty centigrade.' She made a careful note of the reading before looking up, her eyes troubled.

'Dena spoke to the child. It looks as if the onset was pretty sudden.'

'Any vomiting?'

Jan nodded. 'From the way she describes it, I'd say convulsions, too.'

'Has she complained of pain?'

'I think I can manage to ask her that.' In response to gentle questioning, the woman briefly opened her eyes and lifted one blue-veined hand, coughing as she tried to speak.

'It's all right,' Georgia murmured soothingly. 'What did she say?'

'She has pain in her chest, at the back. It's worse when she breathes deeply or coughs.'

'Yes, I'm sure it is.' Georgia uncoiled her stethoscope. 'She's painfully thin, too.' She bent closer. 'I don't want to disturb her more than I have to, but I need to listen to her chest. Can you sit her up and lean her forward slightly?'

With Jan and Dena supporting her, Georgia made a quick but thorough examination. 'Right, you can lay her down again now.'

'Is it tuberculus pleurisy?'

Georgia's fingers felt the rapid pulse in the frail wrist. Straightening up, she shook her head. 'I don't think so. We'll get some blood cultures done and a leucocyte count, but I'm pretty sure that what we have here is pneumococcal pneumonia.'

Smiling reassuringly at the child and gently squeezing the woman's hand, she moved away, leaving Dena to make the patient comfortable. 'We'll get her started on antibiotics straight away. Ideally Ampicillin, five-hundred milligrams, four times a day, or co-trimoxazole, two tablets twice daily.' Writing up the notes, Georgia frowned. 'Do we have either of those?'

'I'll check.'

Georgia nodded. 'Ideally, to give her any sort of fighting chance, she needs cloxacillin as well. The organism isn't likely to be resistant to it. I know. . .' She caught Jan's expression. 'I'm asking for the moon.'

'The prognosis isn't good, is it?'

'On the whole I'd say it's fairly lousy. She doesn't have a lot going for her. She's clearly not old by our standards, but out here. . .' Georgia bit her lip. 'She's severely malnourished so her resistance is probably zero.' She wrote a series of rapid notes and slipped her pen into the pocket of her coat. 'She'll have to be admitted. Let's try and get her started on antibiotics straight away. At least we have to give it a try. Will you arrange to have her taken over to the ward?'

'Will do.' Jan completed her own notes before looking up. 'Where are you off to now?'

Georgia glanced at her watch and gathered up a batch of notes. 'Over to Maternity—I gather there's a bit of a problem; then I'd better put in a ward round. Someone has to cover for Sam and Oz.'

'I hope they're all right.'

Georgia banished a sudden pang of alarm. 'Of course they'll be all right,' she said briskly. 'Gunshot wounds can be pretty nasty, but they're both experienced. They know what they're doing.'

Jan frowned. 'I wasn't thinking of that so much. I was more worried about the guerrillas.'

Georgia felt her throat tighten. 'Surely they'll be long gone? They wouldn't hang around— would they?'

'It's been known. It depends which lot they belong to. In some ways you're better off dealing with the Somalis. They tend to go in for fast raids over the border, then retreat. If, on the other hand, it was the *shifta*. . .'

Georgia looked at her uneasily. 'Sam mentioned them. I think he called them bandits.'

Jan nodded. 'The word actually means outlaw. To put it bluntly, they are killers. The locals may know what goes on but they'll never come forward for fear of reprisals. In a crazy sort of way, they're even admired, unless you happen to be on the receiving end, of course. We've lost countless supplies to them—food, drugs, blankets, you name it. But they don't usually stick around for a fight. Still, as you say, Sam knows what he's doing. With a bit of luck they should be back before dark.'

But what if they weren't? Georgia carried the disquieting thought with her as she made her way across to the ward.

With an effort she pushed the thought away, concentrating instead on the task in hand as the duty nurse came to meet her. Born in India, Ghita Nayer's parents had moved to Britain, where her father was in general practice. Consequently, she spoke with a curious yet enchanting accent which was a cross between Indian and Birmingham.

Aged about twenty-five, she was slim and she wore a white dress with a navy belt. Her smile and quiet efficiency came as an enormous relief to Georgia as the girl led the way towards the women's ward, her pretty face, with its high cheekbones and huge brown eyes, framed by long, jet-black hair which had been neatly braided.

'I gather there might be a problem?' Georgia walked into the small unit reserved for maternity cases. Several of the beds were occupied. Ghita led her to where a young, heavily pregnant girl lay gripping the bed-rail, groaning softly as she tossed and turned. An overhead fan whirred ineffectively and her skin was dotted with perspiration.

'This little girl arrived about two hours ago.' Ghita sponged the girl's brow. 'Is that better? You're still too hot? Here, let me move this sheet. You're tying yourself in knots. There we are. The doctor is here to see you now. She'll soon have you feeling much better.'

'Hello there,' Georgia smiled. 'Are you getting a pain now?' She rested a hand lightly on the girl's abdomen, feeling a contraction build and then slowly fade. 'Oh, yes, that was quite a good one.' In a low voice she said urgently, 'How old is she?'

'According to her notes, seventeen.'

'Well, I suppose it could be true. Is this her first pregnancy?'

Ghita shook her head. 'Fourth. One miscarried, two were stillbirths.'

'Poor child.' Georgia saw another contraction distort the girl's features. Again she waited as it gathered strength, peaked and then faded. 'They're very strong. How long has she been in labour?'

'It's difficult to say.' Ghita bathed the girl's face again and this time offered her a few sips of water. 'She says the pains started yesterday, but the baby isn't due for another four weeks.'

Georgia straightened, frowning, after making a gentle external examination. 'Well, if she's right about the contractions starting yesterday, and I suspect she is, then we could have a problem. She's exhausted.' Her glance strayed to the ancient monitor above the bed. 'There are signs of foetal distress, too. It's all taking too long. Either her pelvis is too narrow or the baby is lying in a breech position. I'll have to do a proper examination but either way she's going to need help if we're not going to end up losing both mother and baby.'

'Dr Sam bring baby.' The grunted words were almost a plea as the girl tried to sit up, only to fall back again, gripping Georgia's hand.

'I'm afraid Dr Sam isn't here right now, but I'm going to help you.'

'Dr Sam. . .he promise me baby.'

Georgia met Ghita's eyes above the mask she had slipped on. 'Do you know what she means?'

'She says he promised that if she came to the hospital this time he would make sure her baby lives.'

Oh, great! Well, bully for you, Sam. Georgia drew in a breath. If you're going to make promises you might at least stick around to see them through.

She took in the girl's restlessness before her gaze shifted again to the monitor. 'This isn't going to wait for Sam. I'll get scrubbed up. Get me a mask and gown,' she said decisively. 'Something's wrong. I need to make a proper examination now.'

A few minutes later she grimly stripped off the surgical gloves. 'I was right,' she said quietly. 'She's never going to make it on her own. The baby is lying at an angle and it's getting pretty distressed. The foetal heart-rate is starting to fall.'

Ghita tugged down her own mask. 'What do you want to do?'

'Well, one thing's for sure—we can't wait for Dr Ryker to get back.'

'You want to do a Caesarean?'

'We don't have any choice. She's already exhausted. If we wait we'll certainly lose them both.' Georgia glanced at the clock. It was later than she had imagined and it came as a shock to realise that it was already dark outside. 'Is there a theatre free?'

'There is, but. . .' The girl hesitated as she helped Georgia out of her gown. 'Dr Moulou is still operating and Dr Ozikwe is with Dr Ryker.'

'Which leaves me.' Briefly, Georgia closed her eyes. Dammit, Sam! Where are you when I need you? she cried silently. 'Get the theatre ready. I'll get scrubbed.'

Fifteen minutes later she found herself looking at the sparsely equipped theatre and felt a moment's panic. What was she doing here? It was all a far cry from the six months' elective surgery she had done before deciding that she would prefer to specialise in medicine. Right now she wished she had made a different choice.

Taking a deep breath, she pulled herself together. 'Right.' She smiled at the assembled team, and glanced at the anaesthetist, who nodded. 'Let's get on with it, shall we?'

In the event it was all over remarkably quickly. Almost before she realised it, she was holding a squirming infant in her gloved hands. 'It's a boy.'

A tiny cry broke the silence as the small scrap of humanity gave vent to nature's most primeval instinct and began to search for food, sucking noisily at its fist. Ridiculously, she felt the tears sting at her eyelids and had to blink them back as she handed the baby to the waiting nurse who took it to be cleaned and weighed.

Suddenly the door of the theatre swung open. A startled cry of protest sprang to her lips only to fade as the gowned figure came closer and Sam's blue eyes met and held hers. A ridiculous feeling of relief surged through her. She felt drained, both physically and mentally, yet at the same time intensely satisfied. The miracle of birth had taken place and she had played some small part in it.

'What the hell is going on here?'

Her hands froze in the act of carrying out what was now a routine procedure. She couldn't believe she had heard the words. Her glance flew up to meet his and she was shocked by the anger she saw in his eyes.

Before she could begin to explain, the baby set up a howl of protest. Sam's gaze swung in its direction and back to her pale face as she stepped, dizzily, back from the table. He was instantly there.

'I'll take over now,' he said brusquely. 'Get some fresh air.'

She went without looking back, the swing door answering to the pressure of her hand as she stripped off her gown and mask, flung her surgical gloves into the bin. Like an automaton she scrubbed her hands under the needle-sharp points of water, then showered and dressed in jeans and a soft blouse, before making her way into the cooling night air, standing in the darkness, willing herself to breathe evenly.

It was time for the evening meal. Lights blazed in the dining-room, smells of cooking wafted across the night air. She had been hungry but suddenly the thought of food seemed to twist her stomach into a knot.

'Damn you, Sam Ryker,' she said aloud, her eyes misted with tears. 'Go to hell and see if I care.'

CHAPTER SIX

THE African night looked like a velvet cloak, yet even now it was beautiful, filled with scents and sounds and movement. Sitting on the veranda steps with her hands clasped round her knees, Georgia stared up at the clear, star-filled sky and, for some inexplicable reason, found it instantly evoked memories of England and of Martin.

In a gesture of frustration she lowered her head against her knees. Why now, when she had imagined her feelings were so well under control at last?

A year ago she had still been haunted by the memory of what she had fondly imagined they'd shared, and the subsequent discovery that she had merely been living in a fool's paradise. It was bad enough that she had allowed herself to be lulled into a false sense of security by sweet words and promises. So often, afterwards, she had cursed her own naïveté. It had taken a long time and a lot of heartache to realise that she hadn't been alone in succumbing to Martin's particular brand of charm. She, who had always prided herself on her level-headedness, had been taken in by an attractive face, by kisses which had seemed to say so much more than words.

Georgia swallowed hard. What they hadn't told her, until it was too late, was that Martin was married, happily married, despite his later protestations. That he even had a child.

She brushed angrily at the tear which rolled down her cheek. She had been lucky to learn the truth—that he was a liar, that he was weak, so weak that even when she had challenged him he had begged her to stay, told her that he would get a divorce.

She might have believed him if she hadn't, quite by chance, seen him with his newly pregnant wife, some weeks later. In a way that had been the catalyst she had needed to make the break, to get right away.

So why, Georgia asked herself, had it all come flooding back now? Perhaps she was simply hankering after the familiar, needed something to ease the feeling of loneliness that had suddenly welled up. Martin had ceased to be a meaningful part of her life some time ago, but she hadn't entirely managed to erase the memories, and they had risen to haunt her now, when she was at her most vulnerable.

Sam's sudden appearance had set off within her a whole chain reaction of emotions—exhilaration after the baby's safe delivery, relief that Sam was safe, exhaustion. The realisation that, apparently,

he still couldn't trust her to do her job seemed
like the final straw in a very long day. Tears of
self-pity welled in her eyes. She dashed them
away, sniffing hard. And to think she had actually
been glad to see him!

'I had a feeling I might find you out here.'

She gasped as the tall figure came towards her
out of the darkness.

'Go away.' Her voice came out thickly. She
blinked the tears furiously from her eyes, conscious yet again of the feeling of physical
attraction she always experienced whenever he
came near. She rose quickly to her feet and Sam
came to a halt in front of her.

'Sulking, Georgia?' he drawled softly.

'I needed some fresh air, to clear my head. It's
been a long day,' she flung at him, 'so if you don't
mind. . .'

'Georgia, wait.' His hands came down on her
shoulders. Seen close to, he looked tired; lines of
strain and tension were etched around his mouth
and eyes. 'I want to thank you for what you did
back there.'

'It was no problem.' She stiffened. 'I was simply
doing my job. In spite of what you may think,
I'm actually rather good at it. And now, if you
don't mind, I really am tired. . .'

His face darkened. She had half turned away
but, infuriatingly, his grip merely tightened, turning her to face him. His touch sent shock-waves

darting through her. She drew a deep breath, her face taut with strain.

'I suppose I deserved that,' he said.

She stiffened, trying to pull away. 'I'd say so.'

He drew a hand wearily across his forehead, then his voice tightened. 'I got back to be told you were operating on one of my patients. I didn't wait to discover the facts.' He drew a breath. 'The truth is, I feel a personal responsibility for Abu, and for a few moments there. . .'

'You assumed I had usurped your authority?' Her gaze levelled with his.

He had the grace to look sheepish. 'When I first saw Abu she had already lost three babies. Not through any fault of her own, but for the lack of proper antenatal care, and what, anywhere else, would be simple, routine procedure. I promised her that if she came to me when the time came for this baby to be born I could give her a live, healthy baby. . .'

'I know. I read the case-notes before I made the decision to operate.' Her chin rose. Despite the turmoil she sensed he was feeling, she was damned if she was going to make this easy for him. 'I had no choice. If I hadn't acted when I did, we might have lost them both.'

His mouth twisted. 'I know that now. I'm sorry, I over-reacted.'

The admission took the wind out of her sails. They stood facing each other like adversaries, yet the tension sparking between them wasn't entirely to do with anger. It was something far more subtle.

Georgia's gaze was drawn to the sensuous mouth, the dark eyes which seemed to be drawing her out of her depth. She could feel the pulse hammering in her throat as she faced him.

'Damn it, you're not invincible, Sam,' she snapped. 'You're human like the rest of us. We do the best we can. Sometimes it's not easy. Sometimes it's downright impossible, but at least we try——'

She broke off as he gripped her arms, hauling her towards him as his mouth came down on hers in a punishing kiss. For several seconds shock held her rigid, then she began to struggle feebly against his more powerful, male strength. This wasn't supposed to be happening. She was angry. She could feel his heart beating. His kiss gentled, soothing her resistance until she moaned softly.

His lips released her, fractionally, to tease her as he found her earlobe. 'I'm sorry. I shouldn't have reacted as I did.'

Her breath spun out on a sigh. 'Don't do this to me, Sam. Damn it, I'm still mad at you.'

'I know.' His gaze explored her features, his finger traced the curve of her mouth and she sighed heavily.

'You haven't even told me what happened today. We were worried.' Her fingers felt the betraying tautening of his muscles beneath his shirt.

His face darkened. 'By the time we got there whoever was responsible for the attack had gone, along with the major part of the supplies.'

'Oh, no.' She looked up at him. 'So what happens now?'

'It makes life more difficult,' he said, and there was a harsh inflexion in his voice. 'It means we'll have to go on sterilising and re-using needles and dressings. It means we'll be short on drugs and we'll have to cut down on food—at least until we can get more flown in.'

'And what about the wounded?'

'It was too late for a couple of the local aid workers. The rest had gunshot wounds or other injuries.' He frowned. 'A rifle butt can be just as effective as the other end.'

She bit at her lower lip. 'You might have been killed.'

'It's a risk that goes with the job.'

'It goes with my job too, Sam.' She broke away, confused and frustrated by a whole gamut of emotions she had never experienced before. 'How is the baby?'

He smiled. 'He's doing fine. He's small but lively.'

'I'm glad,' she said through the sudden tightness in her throat.

Sam's hands came down on her shoulders, forcing her to look at him. To her dismay, tears filled her eyes and she blinked them away quickly.

'Are you all right?'

She nodded. 'I'm fine. I'm tired, that's all.'

He frowned, one finger lifting her chin. 'You're not going all clucky on me, are you, Georgia?'

'Who? Me?' She sniffed and gave a wry laugh. 'Yes. Babies have that effect. It's ridiculous, I know.'

'I don't think so. I'd say it's a very normal reaction.' His mouth twisted. 'Men aren't immune, you know. It isn't an emotion reserved strictly for women. I would have liked to have a child of my own.'

'Oh, Sam.' Her heart went out to him. 'But you still could have. Just because Megan——' She broke off as his blue eyes narrowed.

'Just because?' he prompted softly.

She swallowed hard. 'I'm sorry. Dave mentioned your wife. We weren't gossiping. He just happened to say. . . Sam, I can imagine how you must feel, but you're young. There's still time.'

'No.' Bitterness flared briefly in his eyes.

'But——'

'I don't want to discuss it.'

She looked at him; his face was taut. He still loves her, she thought bleakly. Having children, loving someone else would seem like a betrayal. 'I'm sorry.' She drew a ragged breath. 'I didn't mean to stir up a lot of painful memories. I'd better go.' She had half turned away when he reached out, drawing her into his arms.

'Hey, no, I'm sorry. It's been a hell of a day, but that's no excuse for taking it out on you.' He tilted her face up, then, with a low groan, his mouth came down on hers. 'Oh, Georgia, Georgia.' His thumb caressed the soft fullness of her mouth. 'What am I going to do about you?'

You could love me, Sam, the thought echoed in her brain. But love was an emotion he obviously reserved strictly for Megan. 'I don't know,' she said as she looked up at him. 'But think of something soon, Sam. I'm not sure how much of this I can take.'

His eyes glittered as he wrapped her in his arms. 'I want to make love to you, you must know that,' he whispered against her hair. 'Look at me,' he ordered gently, and, with a supreme effort, she forced her gaze up to meet his. 'God knows, any man would find it hard to resist you, but there's something you should know. I owe you that much. Marriage doesn't figure anywhere in my plans, now or in the future. That doesn't in any way lessen what I feel for you, but don't ask me to make a commitment, Georgia.' He held her from him. 'If you want to walk away right now I won't blame you or try to stop you.'

His eyes were red-rimmed, she noticed. He looked awful. She wrapped her arms around him, snuggling her head against his chest. A muffled groan came from him as he hugged her closer.

'I'm not so easily got rid of, Sam. I'll stay, as long as you want me.' Until you learn to trust me, maybe even to love me, she added silently.

Something flickered in his eyes, an expression of relief, gone so swiftly that she told herself she must have imagined it. He pulled her towards him, his voice muffled against her hair. 'You do know what you're letting yourself in for?'

Right now that was something she preferred not to think about. 'I think I'll take my chances.'

His mouth came down on hers in a kiss that was gentle and undemanding. 'I don't suppose you want to make love right now?'

'I don't think that's a good idea, Sam,' she said huskily. 'I don't think either of us is thinking very straight right now.' She wanted to stay. It needed every effort of will she possessed not to go to bed with him. But she would not be some sort of consolation prize.

'I had a feeling you might say that,' he groaned mournfully. He bent and kissed her again. 'Go to bed, Georgia. Sweet dreams. I'll see you in the morning.'

It was seven-thirty in the morning and there was still a slight chill in the air as Georgia made her way to the hospital. The waiting-room was already full. Outside, a queue had already begun to form and the inevitable group of women gathered round an array of fire-blackened cooking-pots. Within an hour the heat inside the building would be close to unbearable.

'Good morning, Doctor.' Simon N'toto, one of the orderlies, greeted her arrival with a grin. 'The queue is not quite so long today. Maybe everyone get well.'

'It's a nice thought, Simon.' Georgia gave a short laugh. 'It may rain, too, but I wouldn't count on it.'

'Good morning, Dr Maxwell.' Sister Abuna was already at work, taking the names of waiting patients. Smiling, she held out Georgia's white coat.

'Good morning, Sister. Give me a couple of minutes then send in the first patient.' Gathering up the cards, Georgia made her way along the corridor and sat at her desk. She was right about the heat. Midway through the morning there was even a rumble of thunder, but she no longer expected rain. There were too many disappointing false alarms.

Assefa Meskel was fifty years old. Tall and wiry, ebony-skinned, he was dressed in a ragged, one-piece, knee-length cotton garment. He shuffled slowly to the chair, helped by Sister Abuna.

Georgia glanced briefly at the card before looking at him, smiling. 'Can you tell me what is wrong with you?'

The man gestured lethargically towards his legs and then at his hands, making tiny stabbing gestures.

'He says he has little pains.'

'Pins and needles?'

Sister Abuna nodded. 'He complains of numbness.'

'Let's take a look, shall we?' Georgia knelt to make her examination. 'He's certainly very thin, almost anorexic.' She ran her fingers gently over the emaciated limbs. 'There's some oedema here.' Straightening up, she examined his face. 'Mm, here too.' Frowning, she said, 'Ask him if he has any pain or notices any palpitations.'

'He says his heart beats very fast and his legs feel heavy. He has to use a stick to help him walk.'

'Let's have a listen to his chest.' Georgia reached for her stethoscope, looking at the man as she listened to the sluggish sounds of an enlarged heart. 'Yes, well I'd say that what we have here is a classic case of beriberi—a vitamin deficiency.' She frowned. 'Do we have any previous history? He must have been getting symptoms for some time, although the onset was probably so gradual that he may not have been aware of it.'

'I can't find any other notes.' Sister Abuna looked at her. 'Would you like me to speak to his son?'

Georgia brushed her hand gently against the man's skin. It felt cold and she shook her head. 'It may help to explain the treatment, so that he understands the importance of taking the medication.'

Sitting at the desk, she wrote a rapid series of notes. 'I'm slightly worried that we don't know how far advanced the condition is. I suspect his heart is enlarged, chances are he's going into heart failure. On the positive side, the response to treatment is usually dramatically fast. Will you tell him that?'

Sister Abuna translated her words, holding the man's gnarled hand, touching him gently as she spoke, before straightening up. 'He says he is glad. His crops are dying in the fields for lack of rain. If he doesn't bring them in soon, everything will be lost.'

Georgia nodded sympathetically. 'I'm afraid he's going to have to let his son bring in the crops. He must have complete rest. He is to do nothing, absolutely nothing,' she emphasised. 'We'll start him on thiamine, fifty milligrams, intramuscularly. We'll get that started now, Sister, and continue for three days, and follow that with tablets. Ten milligrams, three times a day, until we see a significant improvement.'

It was early afternoon by the time she had seen the final patient and finally managed to finish a ward round. With a feeling of relief she took a quick shower and changed before making her way to the dining-room where she found Jan and Dave and some of the nursing staff already seated and helping themselves to sandwiches.

Easing off her shoes, Georgia sank into a chair. 'Oh, bliss.'

'Busy morning?' Dave asked.

'Is there any other kind?' Sniffing appreciatively, she struggled to her feet again and went to investigate the table where food had been laid out under covers.

'If that's coffee, I'll have mine black, with three sugars.'

She looked up to see Sam standing in the doorway. Khaki trousers hugged his lean hips and thighs, emphasising his maleness. Beneath the thin shirt, his powerful shoulder muscles moved in taut definition. She felt the colour rise faintly in her cheeks as she poured the coffee, willing her hands to remain steady as she handed him the cup.

'You'll be pleased to hear that we operated on that fistula case this morning.'

Refilling her own cup, she said, 'I didn't expect you to be able to fit it in so soon. How did it go?'

'It was perfectly straightforward. All being well, she should be able to go back to her village in a couple of weeks' time.'

'That's wonderful news.'

'Talking of which,' Jan intervened, 'we're taking the truck into town tomorrow, doing the market run. How do you fancy coming along?'

'Market run?' Georgia was suitably mystified.

Smiling, Jan helped herself to another sandwich. 'We have to let our hair down once in a while. It's not entirely a fun jaunt, mind you. Perish the thought!' She grinned at Sam. 'It gives us a chance to collect any mail and to stock up on fresh produce from the market. It helps to eke out supplies a little.'

'It sounds fascinating.'

'It is. Noisy, but definitely fascinating. You should come; you'd enjoy it.'

'I'm sure I would. It sounds great, but I'm on duty.' Georgia shot her a wry look. 'Still, next time maybe.'

'Well, at least think about it. I'm sure something could be arranged.' Gazing out of the window, Jan suddenly leapt to her feet. 'Oz! I've been trying to catch that wretched man all morning. I'm beginning to get the distinct impression that he's avoiding me. Oz!' With a brief wave she was gone.

Draining the last of her coffee, Georgia rose to her feet. 'Time I wasn't here, too. I knew it was a mistake to sit down.'

'Georgia, wait.' Sam frowned. 'You haven't had a day off since you got here.'

'No,' she smiled. 'But then, I didn't expect to. I'm still finding my way around. . .'

'Time off isn't some sort of special privilege,'

he said evenly. 'In this sort of climate and working under these type of pressures, everyone needs some time to relax.'

'It really doesn't matter.' Her smile flicked up at him. 'I'm fine. Besides, I've got mountains of paperwork to catch up on.'

'It's waited this long, it can wait a bit longer.'

'We-ll. I'm certainly tempted.'

'I'm glad to hear it.'

The almost imperceptible pressure of his hand drew her closer. She felt a flood of heat as he stared down at her, felt the deepening intensity of his gaze.

'Oh, but. . .' she glanced uncertainly at him '. . .what about covering here?'

'The round trip will only take a few hours and the likelihood of an emergency developing in the meantime is pretty remote. If it should, then we have sufficient trained staff on duty to cope with it. So, there's no reason why you shouldn't go.' His tone was suddenly brisk. 'We'll be leaving early. Don't be late. I want to make a start before it gets too hot. And don't forget to bring a hat.'

'Yes, Sam,' she murmured after his retreating figure as he strode away, leaving her with the distinct feeling that she had been outmanoeuvred yet again.

He was waiting by the truck next morning when, having slung her bag into the back and cramming her hat on to her head, she climbed into the seat beside him, stifling a yawn as she did so.

Sam grinned. 'Sleep well?'

'Like a log, thank you.' She crossed her fingers, mentally, on the lie. What sleep she did get these days seemed to be punctuated by some disturbingly vivid and all too memorable dreams. 'Just keep your eyes on the road, Sam.'

Humour glinted in his eyes but without a word he started the engine and they headed out into the countryside. For the first half-hour, Jan chattered ingenuously, until the heat and dust became too oppressive for anything other than the most desultory conversation and, after a while, she dozed.

Sam drove in silence, his hands tanned and relaxed against the wheel. Once, surreptitiously, she turned to study his attractive features, noting the damp patches darkening his shirt, and became uncomfortably aware of the trickle of sweat running between her own shoulder-blades. Leaning an arm against the open window, she eased her blouse away from her skin and was devastated to find that he was returning her gaze measure for measure.

He grinned. 'There's a cold drink in the Thermos if you want one.'

Right now a cold shower seemed more appropriate! She shook her head. 'I'm fine, thanks.'

The hillsides and villages were brilliant, picked out in the morning sunshine. Along the dust-dry road, they passed ragged, lean Muslim tribesmen, highlanders dressed in *shammas* and small, skinny children, herding even skinnier goats. A column of donkeys was being driven to the market. The phrase beasts of burden had never had any real significance until now, Georgia thought as she watched them swaying beneath loads of dry grass or earthenware vessels, some so huge that they had be to be carried one to each donkey, dwarfing the poor animal.

Jan woke, yawning and stretching, shortly before they reached Addis Ababa, and craned excitedly out of the window as they edged their way carefully through the congested streets and tracks that radiated towards the town centre.

'Is it always as busy as this?' Georgia asked as they precariously skirted droves of mules and yet more goats.

'Saturday is the big market day.' Sam brought the truck to a halt at last in the market quarter of the town and they climbed out, to be instantly assailed by the heat and noise.

'I'll go to relief headquarters to collect the mail.' Jan's face was prettily flushed and Georgia threw her a glance.

'Oh, but I thought. . .'

'Don't worry,' she grinned, hitching her bag over her shoulder. 'Sam's a far better guide than I am. Safer too, not I think you're likely to come across any trouble. I'll see you both back here in. . .?'

'Better make it a couple of hours.' Sam looked at his watch.

'Fine. I'll see you later, then. Enjoy yourselves.' With a wave she was gone, vanishing into the crowds.

Georgia stared after her. 'But I thought Jan was. . .'

Sam grinned. 'I think you'll find she has other, far more interesting fish to fry. I hate to disappoint you, but I'm afraid you're going to have to make do with me.' He looked her over with swift assessment and said huskily, 'If it's any consolation, I promise not to lose you or to let anything else happen to you—at least, nothing you wouldn't want to happen. Ready?'

'Ready.' She flushed as a glint of humour flared in his eyes. Studiously avoiding his gaze, she jammed her hat down over her hair. 'Where exactly are we going?'

'I wish I could give you the full guided tour. Unfortunately there isn't time, so we'll have to make do with the market, but I'm sure you'll find it fascinating.' Sam held out a hand to steady her as they made their way across the busy road.

'What did you mean,' she said breathlessly as they reached the other side, 'about Jan having more interesting fish to fry?'

He shot her an amused look. 'Didn't you know?' He led her into one of the many narrow alleyways. 'She's engaged to one of the relief workers. He's a teacher.'

'No, I had no idea.'

'I think the engagement is a fairly recent development and still unofficial. Come on, through here.'

It was like stepping into some kind of fantasy land, Georgia thought as she was suddenly hit by sensations, noise, heat and smells, a heady combination of spices and coffee, scents and sounds.

They wandered between rows of stalls offering everything from colourful, locally made rugs to garments. Another area seemed to be reserved for the sale of pots and pans, another for axes and agricultural equipment. There were grass mats, ropes and parasols, saddles and fly-whisks, fruit and vegetables.

Sam fished in his pockets for a handful of coins. 'We'd better take some of those.'

She watched, fascinated, as he spoke to the stall holder, finally exchanging currency for a bag full of oranges and lemons.

'Oh, look.' Fascinated, she stared at beautifully crafted silverware set out on a mat on the ground. She fingered the delicate metal. 'I hadn't realised there were so many different types of cross. Look at this.' She held it up for Sam to see. 'I've noticed a lot of the people wearing the same design.'

'Those are pectoral crosses. You'll find the

Ethiopian Christians wear them, or sometimes a variation called a *mateb*, on a cord.'

The man, crouching on the ground, said something, gesturing towards the goods spread out on a blanket. Sam responded in the man's own language and was met with a sharp exclamation of disgust.

'What did he say?'

Sam grinned. 'I don't think you want to know. Let's just say he wants us to buy something.'

'Well, these necklaces are beautiful.'

'He's also asking what he knows to be a ridiculous price.'

'Oh.'

Sam took the necklace she had been holding and spoke to the man again. The conversation seemed to become quite heated and there was a lot of waving of hands until, suddenly, the man smiled, dropping the necklace into Sam's open palm and accepting several coins in return.

'Come on.' Grinning, he took her hand, leading her out of the crowd. 'Let's get out of here before everyone gets the idea we're a push-over.'

Minutes later they came, laughing breathlessly, to a halt. 'What did you eventually pay him?' Georgia's eyes danced with amusement as she fanned her cheeks with her hanky.

'Probably far more than it was worth.' He took the necklace from his pocket. 'On the other hand, how do you put a value on something like this?

He's spent a lifetime learning his craft. It's probably the only means he has of supporting his family.' He slipped the chain over her head, resting the cross against her throat. He stared down at her and her pulse-rate accelerated dangerously. 'I want you to have this as a souvenir,' he murmured close to her ear. 'Something to remind you of the time you spent in Ethiopia.'

The heat seemed to be having a heady effect on her, Georgia thought faintly. Somehow in the process he had drawn her towards him. She could feel the warmth of his body against hers, smell the distinctive aftershave he was wearing as he cupped her face in his hands, brushing his thumb against her lips.

'I don't think I need a souvenir,' she said unevenly. 'I don't think I'm ever likely to forget.' She looked up to find him watching her, an unreadable expression on his face, heard his soft intake of breath as, gently, he lifted her chin to trace the curve of her mouth. She was beginning to lose control beneath the touch of his hand.

'You're not making this easy, Sam,' she breathed.

'Maybe I don't want to make it easy.' He looked down at her, then, moaning softly, he drew her towards him. 'Why is it that I only have to be near you to want you, to touch you?' His mouth came down, taking possession of hers, the pressure of his kiss deepening in what seemed like a powerful and shocking invasion of her senses.

She heard his sharp intake of breath and desire flared out of control so that, despite herself, she responded. They clung together as his mouth became more ruthless, more demanding. She wanted him with an urgency that shocked her. Her arms reached up, drawing him closer, her fingers twining in the thick darkness of his hair.

His breath fanned her cheek. His lips moved to her eyelids, her throat. 'Oh, Georgia,' he rasped. 'Have you any idea how much I want you?'

How could she not know? 'I love you too, Sam,' she whispered.

She felt him tense, then his head went back as if he was coming up for air. Suddenly, bewilderingly, he was holding her from him. He stared at her, a nerve pulsing in her jaw, then, abruptly, he let her go. 'I didn't mean this to happen.'

She stared at him, disbelief dulling her eyes before she began slowly to fasten the buttons on her dress. 'Sam, what is it? What's wrong?'

He shook his head, breathing hard. 'It isn't your fault. I shouldn't have let things get out of hand.'

Out of hand! Georgia froze. 'Is that what happened, Sam?' she said, her voice catching. 'That's all it was, something that went a little too far?'

'You don't understand,' he said heavily.

She stared at him, tears stinging behind her eyes as she shook her head. 'You're wrong, Sam. I think I do understand, very well,' she said quietly. 'I think I know how you must feel, but there's no reason why you should feel guilty, Sam.' She reached out a hand, pleading with him. 'You're human. It's all right to have feelings. You're not being disloyal to Megan. I know you must have loved her. . .'

'Is that what you think?' His face darkened. 'That this is all some sort of misguided sense of loyalty on my part towards Megan?'

She stared at him, feeling a flush creep into her cheeks. 'Well, yes, but. . .'

'You're way off line, Georgia.' His voice was rough-edged with tension. 'I may feel a lot of things for my ex-wife, but, believe me, love isn't one of them. She destroyed that a long time ago.'

Georgia felt the breath catch in her throat. 'I don't understand.'

He gave a harsh laugh. 'No, I'll bet you still believe marriages are made in heaven and that vows are made to last a lifetime. Well, it may be a nice theory, Georgia, but in practice it doesn't turn out that way. It takes two to make it work.' He turned away but not before she had seen the look of bitterness etched into his features.

'Sam, I'm so sorry. . .'

'Don't be. I don't need your sympathy,' he advised hardly. 'Megan didn't want marriage, she wanted a status symbol and, in her eyes, my being a doctor supplied that need. Oh, it was fine to start with, for a year maybe. That's how long it

took for me to realise what a two-faced, evil bitch
she was.' He turned to look at her and gave a
short laugh. 'My own naïveté where she was concerned still amazes me. I didn't see what was
going on.'

'Sam, you don't have to do this. . .'

His mouth tightened. 'Maybe I *should* have
seen.' He raked a hand through his hair. 'I was
working hard, trying to give her the things I
thought she wanted. I'd just been made a registrar. I was working a ninety-hour week and then
on call, but I thought it was for us.' His mouth
twisted. 'All the time she was seeing someone
else, someone I thought was a friend. . .'

'Don't, Sam, don't.' She reached out to him,
almost choking on the tightness in her throat.

He flinched. 'Don't pity me, Georgia. I don't
need it. I've gone through the pain barrier.'

But she hugged him anyway, holding him tight,
feeling the pounding of his heart. 'Is that why you
came out here?'

'It played a big part in it. After Megan left I
tried settling back into a routine at the hospital,
but nothing was the same. I needed to get away,
to make a fresh start. Then I heard about the work
of the relief agency and saw an advertisement. I
applied and started with a short-term contract.'
He gave a wry smile. 'I just stayed on.'

'You love it out here, don't you?'

His mouth twisted. 'I'd say it's more a love-hate

relationship. On a good day I feel I'm making some progress. On a bad day I wonder what the hell I'm doing here. Nothing I do is really going to change things. I may as well pack up and go home.'

'But you know that isn't true.' She looked at him. 'Abu wouldn't have had a healthy baby if you hadn't persuaded her to come to the hospital. Most of those girls wouldn't be able to go back to their villages, holding their heads high, if you hadn't operated to repair their fistulas.'

'It isn't a one-man band, Georgia.'

'I'm not saying it is, but give yourself a little credit, Sam. Don't be so hard on yourself. You take the responsibility. The hospital couldn't survive without you.'

He gave a slight laugh. 'Are you just a shade biased, Dr Maxwell?'

'We all need you, Sam. You may not realise it, but it's true.'

His gaze narrowed and he drew her closer, holding her against his chest, his hands caressing her hair. 'Right now I think there's only one thing *I* need, and that's you, but I'm not sure I can be what you want, Georgia. I risked everything once, I don't think I can do it again. I meant what I said—marriage isn't an option, not for me.'

An involuntary tremor ran through her as, for an instant, he tensed, then his warm breath fanned her cheek as he feathered kisses against her mouth and the hollow of her throat.

'I want you', he had said. Well, maybe, one day, want could become love. She took his face between her hands and found herself faced with the realisation that it would take no effort at all to fall seriously in love with this man. 'I won't hurt you, Sam. Trust me.'

Her body arched towards him, gasping at the shaft of exquisite pleasure his touch sent coursing through her. There's no future in it, a tiny warning voice rang deep inside her brain. The fact that she was in his arms didn't mean a thing. Making love and being in love were two entirely different things. But without him there was no future either.

CHAPTER SEVEN

'THE good news is that we haven't had a measles case for the past week, so I think we can safely assume that the worst of the epidemic is over.' A loud cheer greeted Sam's words. He raised a hand. 'That doesn't mean we can afford to become complacent.'

'Would we dare?' Dave heckled jokingly.

Sam's brief grin faded. 'I know we all feel like celebrating, but it's going to have to wait. We may have won this particular battle. I hate to use clichés, but in this particular case it applies. The war isn't over and may not be for a long time.' He straightened up from where he had been half sitting, half standing against a desk. 'We're fighting ignorance and prejudice and, in some cases, fear. Attitudes can't be changed overnight. The only way is to educate. Which means we have to keep up the vaccination programme and keep pushing home the message.'

'When do we get to the bad news?' Dave asked.

This time there was a communal groan. Sam nodded. 'You're right. The bad news is that we're running uncomfortably low on supplies. Headquarters know the situation. They're working to

124

get an aid delivery set up, but it could take time.'
He frowned. 'You don't need me to tell you the
kind of pressures they work under, and we're not
their sole priority, much as we'd like to be. We
all need to assess where the greatest need lies.'

'We need to distribute blankets,' Sister Abuna
put in. 'The temperature drops close to freezing
at night now. We also need stocks of basic food
and grain. The harvest is poor again this year.
Even if the rain comes, for many it is already
too late.'

'I know,' Sam said grimly. 'Which is why it's
important to keep on giving out vitamins for as
long as supplies last.' He looked at his watch. 'I'm
due in Theatre. Any more problems or queries?'

'Any news of Geoff?' Jan asked.

'Apparently he's doing well. The heart bypass
seems to have been a success.' Sam gave a slight
smile. 'If I know Geoff he's probably giving everyone hell. I've written to him and included
everyone's good wishes.'

Georgia met Sam in the doorway on their way
out. He was wearing jeans and a short-sleeved
shirt. He planted a kiss on her nose.

'I thought you'd want to know that the mother
you operated on is doing nicely. Baby too. He's
actually starting to gain weight.'

'Oh, that is good news. When will you be
releasing her?'

'In about a week. She needs to build up her

strength before she goes back to her village.' He stood aside to let her go ahead of him. 'Apart from that, the baby is still quite small. I'd like to give it at least a fighting chance.'

'Before the next one comes along, you mean?' she couldn't resist saying, and a faint glimmer of humour lit his blue eyes.

'One miracle at a time is all we're allowed. I think a family-planning revolution may take a while, but we'll get there in the end.' He looked down at her. 'Is it my imagination, or have you been avoiding me?'

She stifled a sigh. Where he was concerned, keeping her distance seemed to be the only way of retaining a grasp on her sanity. She might have known it wouldn't work. 'I've been busy.' She gave a slight laugh. 'We all have, in case you hadn't noticed.'

'I've missed you.'

'I missed you too,' she said softly, feeling all her resolutions to be strong running away like precious water down a drain as he drew her towards him. 'Sam. . .' She glanced quickly round. 'Someone might come in. Did you want something?'

'Oh, yes, please,' he breathed against her hair.

'Sam, I meant it.' She pushed him away, spoiling the effect by laughing. 'You're incorrigible. I don't have time to satisfy your sexual fantasies. I'm supposed to be doing a ward round.'

'Damn! Foiled again.' He gave a mock-sigh then grinned. 'I shouldn't be here either but I did want to see you. No, seriously,' he added. 'I'm due to make a visit to one of the villages later today. It's already been delayed because we were rushed off our feet with the epidemic, but I can't put it off any longer. Will you come with me?'

'I'd love to.' A tiny *frisson* of pleasure ran through her.

'In that case I'll see you later. It's not one of the larger settlements so hopefully we'll be able to get through the vaccinations and a clinic and get back before dark. Oh, and don't forget to bring your bag. You'll be expected to earn your keep.'

'Don't worry, I'll be ready.'

Sister Abuna's usually placid face wore a slightly harassed expression as Georgia entered the children's ward.

'Oh, Doctor, I'm sorry. We seem to be a little behind this morning.' Side-stepping two lively youngsters, she swept one up into her arms and promptly had to field his attempts to relieve her of her headscarf. Speaking firmly in her own language, she threw a wry smile at Georgia. 'You see how it is?'

Georgia laughed. 'Don't worry about it.' She tickled the child under his chin. 'I'd much rather see them all like this than the way they were when they first came to us.' She glanced at the beds.

'I'd say we can let some of them go home, wouldn't you? We'll give them a quick once-over, just to be on the safe side, and see how many of them we can get out of your hair, shall we?'

Sister lowered the child gently to the floor, smiling as she beckoned a nurse who bore him away, making inexplicable crooning noises which drew a look of resignation from the older woman.

For an hour, seemingly indifferent to the noise going on around her, Georgia listened to small chests, checked glands and throats, examined ears, eyes and throats, before finally handing over the last squirming infant and pronouncing, 'Well, as far as I'm concerned, he's as sound as a bell.'

She glanced at the notes, frowning slightly. 'Has he finished the course of antibiotics?'

'Almost.'

'And does his mother appreciate the importance of finishing the medication?' Georgia looked up, smiling at the dark-skinned young girl while Sister Abuna translated.

'She says she understands. She is a sensible little girl.'

'Well, in that case I see no reason at all why she can't take her baby back to her village.' Georgia watched, smiling, as the girl wrapped her baby inside her *shamma*. 'There goes another satisfied customer. We'd better start on the rest now. I'd like to take a look at the little girl who came in a few days ago, with the broken leg. How does she seem?'

Sister bustled along the ward beside her to the bed where the seven-year-old lay sleeping restlessly, fanned by her clearly anxious mother. 'She seems to be running a fever this morning.'

Georgia smiled a greeting at the woman before reaching for the chart at the end of the bed. Scanning the notes, she replaced the clipboard. 'Yes, you're right, her temperature is up.' Frowning, she moved to the side of the bed. As she eased the covers aside to inspect the plaster, her mind rapidly assessed all the possibilities. 'Has she complained of pain?'

'Last night, a little. Nurse thought it might be cramp.'

'Yes, well, that's always a possibility, but it wouldn't cause the fever.'

Georgia deftly made an examination of the child's toes and the plaster. 'Do we know how the break was caused?'

Sister Abuna spoke to the mother. 'She says the child was playing and fell.'

'Mm, well, that foot is showing definite signs of puffiness.' Georgia looked at the notes again, her features marred by a frown of concentration as she studied them. 'It's possible the plaster is simply too tight, but I'm not convinced it's that simple. It's possible there may be an infection caused by any small fragments that may have been

left in the wound. Either that or she simply isn't
responding to the antibiotics.' She tapped the
coiled stethoscope against her open palm and said
decisively, 'We're going to have to take a look.
Sister, can you get someone to give the technician
a call? We'll get a window cut in the plaster so
that we can take a look.'

'I'll do that now, Doctor.' Sister Abuna spoke
to one of the nursing orderlies, who sped away
and, having reassured the child's mother, Georgia
continued her progress along the ward.

She paused at one of the metal-framed cots
where a two-year-old sat coughing and kneading
stressfully at his reddened eyes.

'How's little Gebri this morning? The conjunctivitis still seems to be bothering him.'

'Yes, it is. We try to stop him rubbing his eyes,
but it isn't easy.'

'No, I'm sure it isn't.' Georgia made a play of
tickling the child's chin, at the same time feeling
for enlarged glands. 'Mm, well, those are still
slightly enlarged. What about the cough?'

'It kept him awake for most of the night.'

'Poor little chap. No wonder he's not feeling
too happy.' Georgia reached for her stethoscope.
'I don't want to disturb him unnecessarily, but I
just need to check his chest.'

She listened, frowning, and straightened up.
'Well, I don't think there's any infection there,
but we'll keep an eye on it.' She never failed to

be shocked by the ravages caused by what, back in England, would have been classed as nothing more than a common cold. Out here, where the majority of children were badly under-nourished, their resistance was so lowered in some cases as to be virtually non-existent.

'We'll carry on with the one per-cent ephedrine in normal saline, and let's try benzoin steam medications to see if they ease the congestion.'

It was close to midday before Georgia was finally able to make her way back to her room where she swallowed a quick cup of coffee and headed for the shower. Thirty minutes later, dressed in jeans and a soft, baggy shirt, with her hair, still damp from the shower, tamed into a ponytail, she hurried across the compound to where Sam was loading equipment on board the truck.

'Sorry I'm late,' she managed breathlessly. 'We had a last-minute admission. I thought I was never going to get away.'

'No hassle. I had to load the truck anyway.' For a few seconds his gaze seemed to linger on the figure-hugging jeans she had elected to wear, then he was helping her to climb into the passenger seat.

'Where exactly are we going?'

'It's a small village about an hour's drive from here. I was out there a month ago. This is a follow-up trip.'

Georgia hung on as they set off. 'I hadn't realised quite how wide an area you have to cover.'

He nodded, concentrating on keeping the vehicle steady on the narrow road. 'Obviously we liaise closely with the other relief agencies, so that between us we cover the maximum ground possible.' He frowned. 'Even so, some probably slip through the net. We have to rely on word of mouth to make people aware of the existence of the clinics. Most of them know about the hospital.'

She looked at him. 'I suppose you must meet with some resistance, especially from the older people?'

Sam didn't answer immediately. He needed all his concentration to keep the truck on the narrow track, but she saw him frown. 'I suppose it's inevitable. It's not always resistance; sometimes it comes down to sheer logistics. These people mostly don't possess any kind of transport. The very elderly or the very sick can't walk, so unless they have relatives either willing or able to carry them, sometimes for days, they stay where they are. It's as simple as that. I don't like it, but it's not going to change in the next ten years, maybe not in my lifetime, but gradually, somehow. In the meantime, we just have to pray the aid keeps on coming. It's all we've got, the only hope these people have got.'

Leaning against the window, Georgia wiped her face and eased the weight of her hair from her neck. Without warning the vehicle lurched as a wheel hit a rut, sending her sprawling against him, knocking the breath from her lungs as her body made solid contact with his chest.

She heard him grunt, then his arm came round her shoulders, steadying her. 'I should have warned you, it can be a pretty bumpy ride. The roads give out altogether up ahead, then we're on to tracks. Are you OK?'

For a few seconds she lay against him, gulping in air. He released her to concentrate on the road and she struggled upright. 'I'm fine, thanks.' She caught his grin. 'Just keep your eyes on the road.'

The village was surrounded by parched landscape, and crops of a kind Georgia didn't recognise showed, stunted, through withered brown grass. A small herd of hungry and exhausted cattle grazed on land which needed rain.

'What kind of crops do they grow?' She stared out of the window and Sam followed her gaze as he brought the truck to a halt.

'Mostly barley or bearded wheat.' He switched off the ignition. 'Most people think there's only one rainy season. It isn't true. The main rainy season is July to September, but there are the little rains, too, between February and April. Except that it doesn't always happen that way. We're into March now and it doesn't look as if there's any within a couple of hundred miles.'

She climbed out of the vehicle to stand beside him. Taking off her hat, she wiped her arm across her forehead. 'So what happens if the rain doesn't come?'

His mouth tightened. 'The crops will fail. In a bad year the farmer hardly recoups the cost of the grain he sows.' He reached for one of the boxes, handing it to her. 'This is milk formula, the other box is orange juice and vitamin supplements. We'll set up in that patch of shade over there, by those *tukuls*. Huts,' he said in answer to her unspoken query.

The village was made up of small round thatched *tukuls*, clumsily constructed of stakes and mud, Georgia noticed as they unloaded the truck, watched by a crowd of children who ran alongside them shouting, '*Farange! Farange!*'

'What are they saying?'

'Strangers, or visitors.'

She gave a rueful smile. 'They look an amazingly healthy lot. How on earth am I going to communicate, Sam? The few words of Amharic I've managed to pick up would just about cover 'Can you tell me where the pain is? Anything too technical and I could be in serious trouble here.'

He grinned. 'You could always try sign language. No, seriously.' He beckoned a young girl who had been watching them shyly, hiding her face behind her *shamma*. 'This is Leilt. Over the months we've gradually been teaching the basic rudiments of first aid and midwifery to some of the younger women. Leilt is one of our successes. I'm hoping one day, if her parents will agree, that she'll come to the hospital to train as a nurse. Leilt, this is Dr Maxwell.'

The girl smiled. 'Doctor.'

'I shall be glad of your help,' Georgia told her, 'and, judging from the size of that queue, I think the sooner we make a start the better, don't you?'

By the time they had set up their tables a queue had already begun to form in front of them and within minutes Georgia was smiling reassuringly at her first patient.

The man could have been anything between forty and sixty, and he was painfully thin. He spoke no English, but it was obvious that he was in pain as he limped forward to sit awkwardly on the chair.

Eyeing the soiled rag fastened round his leg, Georgia spoke to Leilt. 'Will you explain to him that I need to remove the dressing in order to examine him before I can help him?'

The girl spoke to the man and looked at Georgia. 'He says you make better.'

'Well, let's hope so.' Carefully removing the makeshift dressing, Georgia had to stifle a gasp of horror at the large, suppurating ulcer which was revealed. Drawing a deep breath, she sat back. 'How long has it been like this?'

'He says he injured his leg several weeks ago, when he was working in the fields.'

'And obviously did little or nothing about it.' Georgia's mouth tightened fractionally as, very gently, she swabbed the ulcerated area before inspecting it again more closely.

'Trouble?' Handing a child back to its mother, Sam leaned over to look and whistled softly through his teeth. 'That looks pretty nasty.'

'I know. I don't think I've seen anything quite like it before.' She looked at him hesitantly. 'Would you mind taking a look?' She moved aside slightly to let him move closer. 'I was thinking of leprosy, but it doesn't follow the pattern. There's no localised loss of sensation, no pins and needles.' She ran a hand through her hair. 'Apparently he injured his leg some weeks ago.'

Sam pulled a wry face. 'And I don't suppose it got even the most basic first aid.'

'My thoughts exactly. In which case I would expect some infection, but this. . .'

'I know what you mean,' Sam murmured, peering more closely at the wound. 'I've seen variations of this.' Frowning, he straightened up. 'I'd say it's myiasis—screw worm.'

Georgia drew in a breath. 'Screw worm. I've seen cases of intestinal myiasis.'

He smiled. 'This is the same little villain, except that in this instance the larvae of the flies have infested the tissue in an open wound rather than settling in the gut. It can affect the eyes, ears and nasal cavities as well, and the damage can be pretty devastating if it's left untreated. The crazy thing is that the treatment is simple and effective. Try an application of ten per cent chloroform in a little vegetable oil. It works wonders.'

'Thanks a lot.' Georgia's eyes flashed her gratitude.

'Think nothing of it. It's all part of the service.'

She pushed a strand of hair from her eyes, feeling dust and perspiration on her skin. The thought of stripping off her clothes and standing under a cold shower rose tantalising in her mind, only to be pushed away as she became aware of him watching her.

With a quick movement she turned away, forcing her attention back to her work. Having scrubbed her hands, she turned to her next patient, smiling at the elderly man who was helped towards the chair by his wife. They both looked thin and ill, but the man was wheezing breathlessly, and clutching at his chest as he produced a dry, rasping cough, leaving a fleck of blood at the corner of his mouth.

Georgia's face registered nothing of what was going through her mind as she spoke to the man, persuading him gently to let her examine him.

Having listened to the low-pitched respirations and typical, laboured breathing of a patient with chronic bronchitis, she dropped her stethoscope into her pocket before reaching for a supply of co-trimoxazole tablets from her bag. Shaking several into a container, she handed them to the man.

'You must take one of these twice a day for seven days,' she explained, waiting for Leilt to translate. 'They will help you to breathe more easily. And I will give you more tablets——' she indicated a second container which she pressed into the woman's hand '——which you should take if the cough returns.'

The man nodded listlessly but the woman grasped Georgia's hands in her own, shaking them before she led her husband away.

Sam was instilling eye drops into a child's badly infected eye as she looked up from completing her notes an hour later.

'Nearly finished?'

'Just about.' Grunting, she eased her back. 'What wouldn't I give for a real cup of tea right now!'

He flashed her a grin. 'Hungry?'

'I could eat a horse. I'd rather *not* but, yes, I'm starving. I missed lunch.'

Stacking away the last of the equipment, he rose to his feet. 'One more patient to see, then we'll eat.'

'Eat?' She stared at him.

'Unless you'd rather not. . .'

'Hey, wait, I'm coming.' She was on her feet, scrambling after him, brushing the dust from her jeans and wrinkling her nose. 'Phew, I could do with a wash.'

Sam grinned. 'I doubt if anyone here will notice. Come on, take a look at the village while we're here. They're all pretty much the same, some slightly larger, but basically everyday life goes on the same way.'

'Oh, look.' Georgia paused to watch a young woman sitting on the ground outside one of the huts. Her breasts were uncovered, and she wore only a thin cotton cloth draped from her waist. 'What is she doing?'

Sam followed her gaze. 'She's churning goat's milk in a skin.' He grinned. 'Want to try some?'

'Er, no, thanks all the same.'

'Where's your spirit of adventure, woman?'

'I left it at Tesco's,' she muttered, falling in beside him, 'and don't say another word. I thought you said you had another patient to see.'

His eyes glinted briefly, sobering again as a tall Ethiopian emerged from the largest hut, beaming as he came towards them, hand extended.

'Dr Sam, welcome.'

'Abba.' Sam clasped the man's hand. 'It's good to be back. This is Dr Maxwell, who has come to work at the hospital.' Georgia felt her hand grasped in a leathery palm. 'Abba Gebri Sellasie is the son of the village head man,' Sam explained. 'His father was very ill with pneumonia, not helped by the fact that he's seventy. I'm hoping a course of antibiotics will have done the trick.'

Stepping inside the *tukul*, Georgia blinked as her eyes adjusted to the shade and the heat. By the open doorway, watched by two small children, a woman was using a skillet to cook over a wooden fire, while another, older woman stirred the contents of a deep jar.

An oil-wick hung on the wall and mud beds were built into alcoves. On one of these sat an old man, wrapped in a *shamma*. The light from the oil-wick glinted on rifles stacked against the wall.

While Sam carried out his examination of the old man, Georgia was motioned to sit and was amused to find herself the centre of attention as the children touched her hair and the women giggled shyly behind their hands.

It was almost a relief when Sam finally stood up, removed his stethoscope and pronounced, 'That's good. The congestion has definitely decreased.' He looked at Abba. 'I'm going to leave some more tablets for your father. He should take them as before.' He waited as the younger man translated.

'My father asked that you stay and eat with us.'

'We shall be honoured, won't we, Dr Maxwell?'

'Absolutely.' Georgia frowned uncertainly at the small, decanter-shaped bottle with a narrow neck which was thrust into her hand. 'What is it?' she muttered under her breath, sniffing surreptitiously, as Sam sat beside her. 'What am I supposed to do with it?'

'Drink it.'

She flashed him a look of disbelief. 'You're not serious?'

'Go ahead. It's called *tej*. It's the local honey-wine.'

She sniffed at it again, raising it cautiously to her lips to take a sip. 'Mm.' She nodded approvingly. 'It's actually very nice, very sweet. But why do they serve it in these strange little bottles?' she whispered.

'They're called *bireles*, and they use them because the narrow necks make it less easy for the flies to get in.'

She swallowed hard. 'Oh, wonderful.' She sighed faintly.

As they watched, the women of the household busily prepared the main meal of the day, and a variety of appetising smells rose to fill the hut.

'Mm, I recognise that.'

'It's *wat*.' Sam accepted a plate as he sat on the floor. 'When you eat, remember to use only your right hand,' he warned. 'You break off a piece of *injara* and use it to mop up a little of the *wat*.'

'Why do I get the feeling I might be going to regret this?'

The woman sitting by the wood fire lifted a conical pottery lid from one of the large jars, instantly releasing another, very strange smell into the hut as, with a filthy rag soaked in vegetable oil, she wiped the skillet before pouring on to it the fermenting, grey-coloured batter she scooped from the jar.

Georgia closed her eyes, feeling her stomach tighten. She watched as the batter spread and cooked until it looked like a thin pancake which was then folded and handed to her. With an effort she forced a smile. 'You know, suddenly I'm not so hungry.' She held up a hand as the contents of a large dish was proffered. 'I think maybe I'll give it a miss, if you don't mind.'

'Eat it, Georgia,' Sam drawled, smiling, as he reached over and ladled a generous helping of *wat* on to her plate.

She gulped hard. 'I can't. I'm not. . .'

'You can and will.' His smile was fixed. 'A refusal to eat what is offered will be considered an insult. You'll eat it if I have to force it down your throat, Dr Maxwell.'

'I hate you,' she spat. 'If I die of food poisoning I shall hold you personally responsible.' She gave him a fierce look which he totally ignored as he broke a piece of *injara*, mopped up some of the sauce and held it to her mouth.

'Eat and smile.'

Her lips tightened. 'Have you seen the state of that. . .cauldron?' she said through gritted teeth. 'It's positively unhygienic.'

He raised one dark eyebrow. 'That's because

injara jars are never washed. The scraps of stale dough sticking to it help to speed up the fermentation of each fresh mixture.'

'I don't believe this is happening to me.' She smiled, swallowed and gasped as the fiery combination of peppers and chicken brought tears to her eyes. In desperation she reached for the *tej* in an attempt to cool her mouth, only to find it burned even more fiercely. 'Oh, God, I'm dying.'

'You'll get used to it,' Sam drawled as he helped himself to more.

'I should live so long.' She dashed a hand across her streaming eyes and nose; his silent laughter enraged her. 'I won't forget this, Sam, I promise you.'

His shoulders shook.

The truck loaded, they took their leave about an hour later, and not a minute too soon, Georgia thought as, rejecting his outstretched hand, she scrambled with undignified haste to her own side of the seat and sat, glaring, out of the window.

Grinning, he set the truck in motion, along with the wheels grinding inside her head. She didn't know which was going to prove more lethal, the honey-wine or the lingering aftermath of the meal. Either way, right now, death seemed like a sound option.

At least it grew cooler as the sun slid with remarkable speed below the horizon, and she was glad of the darkness which made it marginally easier to ignore the effect Sam's nearness was having on her nerves.

'You're not still sulking, are you? It's a long way back to camp, Georgia. I could do with some company around here.'

'You don't deserve it.'

Even in the dark she caught the feral gleam in his eyes as he turned to look at her. 'You're right, I probably don't. On the other hand,' he said evenly, 'those people barely have enough food for their own survival. . .'

'Oh, great.' She winced as her head throbbed. 'If this is supposed to make me feel better, I can tell you now it's not succeeding. So what were we doing back there? Helping them out by eating a month's rations?'

'Georgia.' He reached out a hand and she stiffened.

'Don't talk to me,' she sniffed. 'My mouth's still on fire.'

She heard him chuckle softly. 'I'll admit, it takes a little getting used to.'

'A little! Has anyone ever told you you're a sadist, Sam Ryker?' Her glare of fury became one of wariness as he brought the truck to a halt a short distance from the hospital, and cut the ignition. 'What are you doing?'

He leaned back in his seat, stretching his arms. 'Trying to unwind, trying to say I'm sorry.' He waited a moment and when she didn't respond

he said quietly, 'Those people have their pride.
To have refused their hospitality would have been
an insult.' His lean fingers fastened gently on her
arm to draw her towards him and when she would
have pulled away his other hand came up to tilt
her chin. 'Hey, come on now, was it really so
bad?' His mouth twisted. 'I suppose I've got used
to it. After a while it sort of grows on you.'

'I can believe that,' she muttered, 'having seen
what was bubbling away in those jars. No——'
she looked into his eyes and felt her heart turn
over '——I know what you're saying. I over-reacted.
I knew it was going to be different. I just wasn't
prepared for how different.' She gave a rueful
smile. 'And I still feel as if my mouth's on fire.'

'In that case, perhaps I'd better kiss it better,'
he said gravely. As he looked into her eyes, his
hands tightened fractionally on her shoulders.
Then, when she offered no resistance, he caressed
her flushed cheek, drawing her towards him. 'I've
been wanting to kiss you all day,' he breathed
against her hair as she relaxed against him with
a sigh.

His head began a slow descent. She took his
face between her hands, meeting his eyes, willing
him to love her. His mouth brushed against her
eyelids, her cheeks. He moaned softly, 'Oh, God,
I want you,' then his lips came down tenderly
on hers.

His hands raked through her hair, moved to

her shoulders, following the curve of her breasts, sending a shaft of exquisite pleasure coursing through her. She groaned as he pushed aside the soft fabric of her blouse.

'Love me, Sam,' she whispered into the darkness, her head going back as his mouth strayed to her throat, and lower and. . .

'Oh, my. . .!' She froze, feeling him tense as he looked straight into her eyes.

'Georgia, what. . .?'

She stared past him into the darkness. 'The hospital,' she rasped, frantically tugging her blouse together. 'There's a fire, Sam. The hospital is on fire! People could be trapped!'

CHAPTER EIGHT

GEORGIA didn't wait to see if Sam was following her. Thrusting the door of the truck open, she was already running, heading for the compound where a thick column of grey smoke billowed into the air and the sound of screams drove her on.

Ten yards from the timber out-patients' block, she was forced to a halt as the thick, acrid smoke caught in her throat. Shielding her face with her arm against the heat, she stared helplessly into the flames. Several figures were running and she wished the thick, choking curtain would disperse so that she could see to get to where help was most needed.

'It's the out-patients' clinic.' The air rasped in her lungs as she coughed, pressing a hand over her nose and mouth, desperately trying to get closer, inching her way forward. 'All the equipment, the records,' she almost wept.

'Go and get help.' Sam was beside her, dragging off his shirt, beating at small tongues of flame which were beginning to spread with frightening speed.

'Help is already on its way,' she called, brushing her arm over eyes that smarted from sparks and the gathering intensity of heat. 'Someone could be trapped inside.'

'It's not likely. I'm going in through the window. Get the hell out of here,' Sam's voice cracked through the darkness, and she ignored it. People were running from all directions, only to be driven back by the flames.

Vaguely she was aware of Dave, heard him yell, 'Where's Sam?'

'He's going inside.'

'Jeez!'

From the end of the building came a loud splitting of wood as she turned her head in time to see orange flames licking and curling at the dry timbers. There was a sudden hiss of air as the roof caught alight. 'Oh, no!' She felt cold tears of despair run down her cheeks. This couldn't be allowed to happen. Everyone had worked so desperately hard; so many people depended on the clinic. Somehow something had to be saved.

Heat scorched her arms as she edged her way closer, trying to reach the door where smoked billowed, but the flames hadn't yet reached. Ducking down against the heat, she pushed with her foot but nothing happened and she almost wept aloud with frustration. Of course, it would be locked.

'Come on, come on.' She struck out again. At the second blow it gave and she almost fell inside, gasping as the heat and smoke hit her like a huge, suffocating wave. On her knees she crawled forward, feeling with her hands for the wall which, she hoped, would lead her to the main storage area.

A timber snapped somewhere overhead. A scream welled up, dying in the burning dryness of her throat as her hand came up against another door. She flinched as the heat seared her skin, then, with a tiny whimper of relief, she pushed at it and felt a pair of hands snake round her waist, dragging her backwards.

'I told you to get out of here,' Sam's voice rasped out of the thick, choking smoke. 'Go, *now*. The roof could fall in any minute.'

She pushed him away. 'I'm not going anywhere while there's a chance we can save some of the equipment.'

'Damn the equipment! I want you out of here now.' Sam made a grab for her, lifting her bodily. She fought him, lashing out blindly.

'Let me go.' She heard him swear as her foot made contact with his shin.

'Damn it, don't make me hit you. If that's the only way. . .'

'You're wasting time.' She beat at him with her fists, giving a tiny cry of triumph as he relaxed his hold long enough for her to swing away from him. He rocked back and one of the roof timbers crashed down, catching him a glancing blow on the temple.

Georgia stared, horrified, as he reeled, then saw with relief that he was still on his feet. Coughing on the smoke-filled air in her lungs, she turned back towards the door, had almost made it when his steely grip locked on her shoulders. Her cry of frustration mingled with the roar of the fire as she struggled to break free.

'You crazy little fool.'

She caught a brief glimpse of his expression, grim and uncompromising, before she was slung unceremoniously over his shoulder and carried, beating furiously at his back as he staggered towards the door.

He thrust her into Dave's arms. 'Hold on to her. Keep her here.'

She could only stand, watching helplessly, as he turned back and, within seconds, was swallowed up in the smoking inferno.

'We can't just stand here. We have to do something,' she pleaded with Dave.

'There's nothing we can do,' he said tautly. 'The building's already as good as gone. At least no one was inside. Clinics had finished for the day. It could have been a hell of a lot worse.'

But not much, she thought, and it wasn't over yet. Sam was still in there.

She sagged against Dave as reaction began to set in. Red-eyed, she peered through the smoke, waiting for Sam's reappearance, and it was only when he finally emerged, coughing and smoke-blackened, carrying out the metal drugs box, that Georgia felt the leaden bands of tension snap inside her. He was safe; that was all that mattered. But he could so easily have died in there, never knowing how very much she loved him.

Like an automaton she started walking towards him. It seemed like an oddly uphill climb, as if her feet were being held by heavy weights. Sam looked grim-faced. There was a livid gash on his forehead.

'You're hurt.' Instinctively her hand went towards it.

He recoiled, catching hold of her wrist. 'You crazy little fool. What the hell did you think you were trying to do? You deliberately disobeyed my order. I suppose you realise you might have been killed in there?'

'I didn't think.' She stared at him, confused by his anger.

'No, I don't suppose you did.'

'But someone had to get the equipment out.'

'Equipment can be replaced,' he ground out.

She tried to laugh but it came out as a cough and she felt her head swim. Instantly his hands were on her arms. She flinched. Sam was on to it in a flash, his mouth tightening as he stared at the reddened area.

'You're hurt,' he said in a quietly controlled voice.

'So are you.' She tried in vain to draw her arm

away, the sudden movement making her cough all over again.

'I'll live,' he rasped. 'Come on, let's get this seen to.'

'But we can't. . .'

'There's nothing more we can do here. The building's gone but at least no one was seriously hurt.'

She stared dizzily at him. 'But how did it start?'

'We'll probably never know. Everything is as dry as tinder. The sun could have reflected on a piece of glass, a spark from one of the cooking fires, who knows. . .?'

She coughed again and his hands cupped her face, forcing her to stare straight into his eyes. 'You're exhausted, probably suffering from shock too.'

He looked pretty exhausted himself, she thought as he looked down at her, his jaw tensed, a nerve pulsing in his throat. Ridiculous tears welled up in her eyes. He put her firmly from him just as she strained towards him. 'You need to have those burns looked at. You've inhaled a lot of smoke, too. Here, you'd better hang on to me.'

Wearily she studied his expression. There seemed no logical reason for the brief glimpse of anger she had seen reflected in his eyes.

'I can manage.' Stubbornly she pulled away and instantly regretted it as the ground seemed to spin beneath her feet. She heard him swear softly then, before she knew what was happening, he had swung her up into his arms. She tried to protest but weariness washed over her.

She was scarcely aware of him pushing open the door of her bungalow, or depositing her gently on the bed. It must be the aftermath of tension, she told herself, a release of a whole lot of pent-up emotions. For a while she had imagined Sam would die. Suddenly the enormity of what that would mean hit her full force and she began to shake uncontrollably.

As if to wipe out the memory of the burning building, she rubbed the back of her hand across her eyes, then stared blankly at her smoke-blackened fingers.

Sam had moved. She started as a glass was thrust into her hands. 'Here, drink this. I wouldn't normally recommend it for shock, but right now I think you need it.'

She sniffed at the amber liquid and recoiled. 'I don't like brandy.'

'Drink it,' he ordered impatiently, then, with a muttered oath, he was beside her, steadying her trembling hands with his own.

She took a sip, choking as the fiery liquid burned her throat, and pushed the glass away. 'I'm fine, really, just a little shocked. So much damage. . .' Her voice trailed away on a note of disbelief.

'It could have been worse. It could have been one of the wards.' He looked at her for a few seconds before he cupped her face, forcing her to look at him. 'You crazy little idiot.'

'Idiot yourself.' She sniffed hard.

'Have you any idea of the kind of hell you put me through, rushing in there like that?'

He had gone through hell? Where did he imagine she had been? To hell and back ten times over.

She closed her eyes as his mouth came down on hers with a need that drove the exhaustion away, before he put her gently from him. 'We should treat that arm. Georgia, don't.' He groaned softly when she strained towards him. 'Right now neither of us is thinking straight. You need a shower and to get some sleep, in that order.'

She bit her lip in an effort to stop the tears that suddenly welled up into her eyes. As he tilted her face to kiss her again, he saw the tears on her cheeks. 'Oh, God, Georgia, my darling, don't.'

'What I need most of all is for you to hold me, Sam. I just don't want to be alone right now.' Her green eyes raised to his. For a second she saw the conflict raging within him, then, with a low groan, he came to her and she swayed against him, breathing deeply. His body was warm and hard and strong.

'This is crazy,' he muttered. 'You're in a state of shock. Do you have any idea what you're doing?' His voice roughened and she looked up at him, her head tilted so that her honey-blonde hair spilled over her shoulders.

'I'm not sure that I care,' she told him huskily. 'All I know is that I might have lost you and I don't think I could bear that.'

'Oh, Georgia. . .' He broke off as her hands travelled up, over his arms, feeling the tension in him.

She could feel the powerful strength of his hands through the thin fabric of her blouse. A tiny, purely involuntary shiver of desire ran through her. 'Stay with me,' she whispered. 'I love you, Sam.'

She heard his sharp intake of breath. 'Oh, God, I want you. . .' His lips came down on hers in a heated, sensual demand, the urgent, seeking pressure of his mouth releasing a fiery compulsion that burned deep within her, a passion that cried out for satisfaction.

Her head tilted back as, gently, he dealt with the buttons of her blouse, pushing the material aside. She gasped as his fingers sought and found the soft swell of her breast. She clutched at his shoulders, faint with a helpless yearning. 'Don't go, Sam, don't leave me.'

'Georgia.' His hand cupped her chin, forcing her to look at him. 'Are you sure, my darling?

Do you know what you're asking? I can't change what I feel. . .'

Her own need was released in a moan of frustration as he gently held her from him. His breathing was ragged, uneven.

'If I stay I'll take you to bed and make love to you.'

'It's all right, Sam,' she whispered as he gathered her up into his arms. 'It's all right. I'll take whatever is on offer. I love you. I won't ever hurt you.'

She woke early next morning, her hair tousled, a smile on her lips as she reached out to the warm space beside her. It was empty but there was a note on the pillow.

Good morning, sleepyhead. You were snoring so soundly, I hadn't the heart to wake you. I have to do a ward round, but I'll catch up with you later. Thank you, my darling.

With a sigh she snuggled into the warm hollow where he had lain beside her. It still smelled of him, of their lovemaking, of the demands they had made of each other and given freely in return. 'Oh, Sam,' she sighed, hugging the pillow to her. 'I do love you, and I know you love me, even if you're not quite ready to say it.'

Stretching and stifling a yawn, she opened one

eye to peer at the clock and, with a yelp of dismay, leapt out of bed. 'Sam, you beast, you switched off the alarm. And how am I supposed to explain my late arrival?'

As it happened, she didn't have to. Thirty minutes later, showered and dressed in a light cotton shirtwaister, she made her way over to the ward, the air still tainted by smoke, where Jan greeted her arrival with a look of astonishment. Deftly cocooning a squirming infant in a towel, she proceeded to bathe its sticky eyes. 'What on earth are you doing here?' She looked up, reaching for a fresh cotton-wool swab. 'Sam said he'd ordered you to have a lie-in after last night.'

'H-he did?' Georgia felt the heated colour surge into her cheeks.

'That's right. He popped in earlier. There now, little man, that wasn't so bad, was it? Now, let's deal with the business end, shall we?' Unwrapping the baby, she lowered him gently into the water, steadying the flailing limbs before she looked at Georgia. 'He said you were still suffering from shock.'

Well, that was certainly true, Georgia thought. Shell-shocked might be a good word to describe how she was feeling right now. 'I'm fine, really. There's no need for anyone to make a fuss.' She made a business of hunting for a pen and missed the look of amusement her friend shot in her direction.

'After what you did last night, at the fire, I'd say a lie-in is the very least you deserve.'

Georgia frowned. 'I don't think I achieved very much.' She riffled through the first batch of cards. 'Sam deserves all the credit for getting most of the equipment out. He and Dave between them seem to have managed to salvage pretty well everything, including me.' She smiled wryly.

'It was lucky it was confined to the one block and didn't spread. It all looked pretty close. I was gearing up to move all the patients out. It could have been a lot worse if a clinic had been going on at the time.'

'I know,' Georgia sighed. 'Talking of which, I suppose it's time I made a start. Anything particular I should know about?'

Jan handed the infant over to a waiting orderly. 'There you go. All he needs now is a good feed.' She turned her attention back to Georgia, the two of them walking up the ward together. 'Nothing urgent. Things are easing off now that we've seen the last of the measles cases, thank goodness.' Pulling a face, she touched wood.

'I know what you mean.' Georgia smiled. 'What about the little girl who went down to Theatre to have a hole cut in her plaster? Ah, yes. . .' They paused at the foot of the bed where she reached for the clipboard. 'I see her temperature is responding to the new antibiotics. Well, that's certainly good news.'

'Yes, she's much better, aren't you, Susi?' Jan plumped pillows. 'You were right about the infection. It could have been nasty.'

'It's lucky it was spotted in time.' She smiled at the child. 'A few more days and you can go home. Let's hope they're all as easy as this,' she added to Jan.

They moved towards the next bed. 'And this is Gebri.'

'Yes, I remember, the little chap with the very nasty cold.' Georgia sat on the edge of the bed, looking at the child's eyes. 'Mm, the conjunctivitis has cleared. How does he seem otherwise?'

'Actually, he's much brighter today.'

'Let's just have a quick listen to his chest, then, shall we? Oh, yes, much better. Throat?' Georgia gave a tiny mock-gasp as she peered into his mouth. 'Oh, my, yes, I think that's definitely ready to go home.' She ruffled his hair. 'Tell his mum he's doing nicely.'

Fanning her cheeks against the warm air, which still bore faint traces of wood smoke, Georgia made her way steadily from bed to bed, listening, carrying out examinations, talking to anxious mothers.

It was another hour before she finally completed the round. 'I think we'd better take a look at our new mums and ladies in waiting.' She walked into the small maternity unit and was greeted by smiles from the women, most of whom were heavily pregnant. Others, sitting beside their beds, nursed their babies.

'Things are pretty quiet at the moment.' Jan led the way.

'Don't tempt fate,' Georgia grinned. 'It could just be the lull before the storm.' Making her way to one of the beds, she smiled at the girl sitting in the chair. 'Abu, you won't remember me. . .'

'Yes, I remember. You bring my baby.' The girl rocked the infant who sucked noisily on his fist as she rocked him in her arms.

Georgia gave a slight laugh. 'Yes, well, I suppose I did, although Dr Ryker was there too, as soon as he could be. How is the baby?'

Ghita Nayer topped up a jug with fresh water. 'He's doing very nicely. In fact, he's a little gannet, aren't you, young man?'

'Is that so? Well, let's take a look at you. Come on, then, up you come, my cherub.' Georgia hoisted him up, supporting his tiny head as she rocked him gently against her shoulder.

'Makes you feel quite broody, doesn't it?' Jan grinned. 'Dangerous little things, babies. I've heard they're catching.'

'Wishful thinking?' Georgia smiled.

'Well, I must admit I wouldn't mind the odd one or two cluttering up the place.' She brushed a finger against the baby's velvety cheek. 'How about you?'

'Me?' Georgia craned her neck to gaze at the

tiny scrap of life nuzzling at her face and felt
her throat tighten spasmodically on the sudden
realisation that she wanted a child of her own,
Sam's child, growing inside her. 'Yes,' she said
huskily. Her breath caught in her throat, the right-
ness, the certainty of her own need suddenly
overwhelming so that when she turned slowly, to
see Sam standing in the doorway, the look in
her eyes was like an unspoken message and she
whispered breathlessly, 'Oh, Sam.'

She stared at him, feeling the pulse hammering
in her throat as she remembered the naked silki-
ness of his body twined with hers, the hot,
sweating passion with which they had discovered
each other and finally made sweet, wonderful
love, so that she looked at him now, feeling the
warm colour surge into her cheeks. How long had
he been standing there? she wondered, a sensuous
smile on her lips.

Then something about the way he was looking
at her made her catch her breath. There was no
answering gleam of understanding in the dark eyes
which looked into hers with such deadly calm
now. Instead, for a moment, she imagined it was
almost pity she saw there, except that she knew
that couldn't be right.

She smiled, her hand instinctively stroking the
baby's tiny back. 'I'm afraid I got a little side-
tracked here. I'm just on my way. . .'

The thick, dark brows drew together. 'I'd like

to see you in my office, Dr Maxwell, at once.'

She stared at him. His tone was icy, unrecognisable as that of the man who had made love to her only a matter of hours ago, and, unconsciously, she flinched.

His steady gaze narrowed and she was aware of a terrible feeling of vulnerability, as if a barrier had come down between them, shutting her off, and she was in some way to blame.

Watching him stride away, she felt a sudden wave of nausea in the pit of her stomach and knew that her face was white as the colour drained from it.

She handed the baby back to his mother, made her excuses before heading for the office. The door was closed. She walked in without knocking, a smile on her lips.

'Sam?' Her voice seemed to be stuck somewhere in the dryness of her throat. 'Sam, what is it? What's happened?'

He turned slowly to stare at her. His appearance shocked her. He looked haggard and for one moment she was able to convince herself that there was a look of pain in his eyes before it vanished and he took a step towards her.

'Dave will be taking the plane out to pick up fresh supplies some time during the next week,' he said flatly. 'I want you to be on it. Your job here is finished.'

CHAPTER NINE

GEORGIA stared at him, feeling the colour drain from her face. 'Sam, what are you saying?'

He turned to look at her, his expression darkening. 'I don't know how to put it more clearly. I'm terminating your contract. Your presence here is no longer required.'

Georgia was shocked. This was like a nightmare; she couldn't believe it was happening. Any minute now she would wake up and find it was all a dream, except that she knew it wasn't.

'But. . .I don't understand,' she whispered. A feeling of nausea crept through her. She looked at him and it was like seeing a stranger. How could this be happening? The warmth and happiness of only a few hours ago seemed to be falling apart, shattered like fragile glass. She took a step towards him and he turned away. 'Sam, you have to tell me what's wrong. Is it something I've said, or done? If so, at least give me a chance to put things right.'

'There's nothing to discuss. Surely it's simple enough. I want you out of here.'

Georgia swallowed hard on the lump in her

throat. 'Sam, this is not making sense. . . Talk to me. Don't I at least deserve that? Don't just freeze me out. Tell me what's happened.'

He paced away, ignoring her outstretched hand, turning to glare at her. 'As if you don't know. My God, did you really imagine I was so naïve?' His voice rose. 'I told you. I warned you. What happened? Did you think it was all some sort of game?'

She shook her head numbly. 'I don't know what you're trying to say. . .'

'You knew the rules.' His voice was bitter. 'I told you, I warned you that marriage wasn't part of my plans, but you didn't listen, did you? Or did you just imagine I could be lulled into a false sense of security by a quick. . .?'

'Sam, don't say it.' The feeling of nausea deepened, creeping through her, twisting her insides. 'If this is about last night. . .' She shook her head, trying to clear the fog that seemed to be clouding her brain. 'What happened happened because we both wanted it.' She stared at him, willing the tears not to fall. 'Or was I mistaken, Sam?' she said quietly. 'We made love. I thought. . .'

'What?' He laughed bitterly. 'I told you not to count on me, Georgia. If you want to play happy families you'll have to find someone else, someone who believes in roses round the door and happy ever after.' His face was flushed with anger. 'I said marriage wasn't part of my plans; it didn't occur to me that I should have said the same goes for children.'

So that was it. She took a deep breath. 'I can't believe you mean that,' she whispered, 'not after. . .'

'Then you'd better start believing it.' He was deadly calm now. 'What happened between us changes nothing.'

'You're saying. . .' Her voice broke. 'You're saying it was just a one-night stand? Is that it?'

His face contorted with what looked like pain, but it was gone so swiftly that she told herself she must have imagined it. 'That rather depends on you.'

Georgia closed her eyes briefly, then forced herself to look at him. 'It doesn't have to be like this, Sam. I know you've had a bad time but I wouldn't do anything to hurt you. . .'

'It's a risk I'm not prepared to take.'

She sighed. 'I'm not Megan, Sam.'

He looked at her with narrowed eyes. 'You don't know the first thing about my wife.'

'I know what you told me. . .'

'I told you she was a bitch. That's true. But what I didn't tell you was that she killed my child.'

She gasped as if someone had physically punched her in the stomach. 'Oh, Sam, no.'

His mouth twisted. 'Oh, I don't suppose any court would call it murder, but that's how it felt to me.' He paused, struggling for control. 'She was pregnant when she walked out, and yes, it was mine.' He gave a short laugh. 'One of our attempts at a reconciliation. I must have been crazy to think it could have made any difference.'

Georgia licked her dry lips. 'What happened?'

'She wrote to me a couple of weeks later, telling me that she'd had an abortion. She hadn't seen fit to consult me since I was no longer part of her future. God knows what story she concocted for the doctors.'

'Sam, don't. . .' She reached out a hand and saw him flinch.

'I don't want your pity. Children had no part to play in Megan's scheme of things. Who knows?' His mouth twisted. 'Maybe it was for the best. She would never have wanted it or cared for it. But I'm not going to go through that again.' He turned to look at her. 'Don't think I'm not tempted; I am. Unfortunately, in the cold light of day we might both regret it, and it's a risk I'm not prepared to take.'

'Aren't you being a little unfair?' she said sharply. 'Just because things went wrong once, it doesn't mean they will again.' There was a tremor in her voice as she said, 'It doesn't have to be that way, Sam. Why won't you at least give us a chance to work things out?'

He gave a short laugh. 'You can't change what you are, Georgia, any more than I can. You want, *deserve* all the things I'm not prepared to give you. You should have children. Unfortunately they won't be mine, but that's the price I'm prepared to pay.'

And what about me, Sam? she thought as the door closed behind him, leaving her to battle with the sobs that were suddenly tearing at her throat. What about me? Can't you see, you great fool, that I love you and if I can't have your babies then I don't want them at all?

But that was the trouble, wasn't it? She pressed a hand to her mouth. Making love and being in love were two very different things. She had made the mistake of confusing them, and it was no consolation telling herself that she would have settled for either. Sam wasn't giving her the choice.

Three days later, the early morning sun was beginning to shift the night's chill as she made her way down the steps and across the compound.

Shivering momentarily, she paused to stand drinking in the breathtaking beauty of the start of another African day. There was a special kind of magic about it that, no matter if she lived here a lifetime, she knew would never fade.

A low mist hung over the distant trees. Leaning against the rail, she watched the wary movements of an animal taking advantage of the coolest part of the day to hunt. There was a cruelty about it, but then, nature was cruel. The whole of life was a matter of survival of the fittest. The youngest, oldest, the sick, all fell prey. Overhead, a bird circled like a dark shadow on a rising current of air.

The sky was a cloudless, searing blue. Within half an hour its heat would be relentless. At the far edge of the compound, Dave was working under the bonnet of the truck. He looked up, smiling, as she approached.

'Problems?' she asked.

He straightened, wiping his hands on an oil-stained cloth. 'Just a last-minute check. You can't take chances out here. Everything's loaded. We should be ready for the off in a few minutes.'

Georgia shaded her eyes against the sun. 'I gather we've had word of some kind of epidemic at one of the villages about forty kilometres from here. Any idea what?'

He shook his head and she followed him to the rear of the vehicle, checking the packages and handing him an insulated box. 'These are the vaccines. I read the radio report. Mainly sickness and diarrhoea. It sounds as if the whole village could have got hold of some contaminated meat.'

'It happens.' Dave slammed the bonnet down, but made no attempt to move. 'Look, are you OK? Only I heard. . .about Sam. I think he's crazy but. . .'

'Yes, I'm fine.' She forced a laugh, and wished she hadn't as it unleashed a myriad emotions she was trying so desperately to hold in check.

Blinking hard, she busied herself unnecessarily, making sure the equipment was safely stowed. 'I have to admit I'm going to miss this place, all the friends I've made.' She turned to face him, biting hard at her lower lip. 'Do you have any idea when. . .when we'll be flying out?'

'A couple of days from now. A load of emergency aid has come in. I'm supposed to pick it up.' Dave took her in his arms, holding her as she fought to bring her feelings under control. 'If it's any consolation,' he said gruffly, 'deep down I'm sure Sam doesn't want to lose you.'

She sniffed hard. 'He has a very funny way of showing it. It's just as well I'm replaceable.'

'The trouble with Sam is he can be his own worst enemy.'

'Funny.' She gave a short laugh. 'I got the distinct impression that honour was strictly reserved for me.'

Dave's face twisted. 'Maybe you're the only person who's come anywhere near to offering any kind of threat.' He took her bag from her, lifting it on to the seat. 'Sam may be a friend of mine, but there are times when I'd like to beat some sense into that thick skull of his.' He bent, smiling, to kiss her, then sobered. 'Personally I think he's all kinds of a fool.'

'You're a nice person, you know that?' She laughed, feeling suddenly awkward, and looked at her watch. 'We'd better get going, or neither of us is likely to be flavour of the month around here.'

He grinned. 'Why do women always change the subject when they're cornered?'

'It's called self-preservation. Come on, let's make some distance before it gets too hot to bear.' She was glad when he responded to her deliberately light-hearted attempt to change the subject, and minutes later they were heading away from the compound, the truck bouncing over the dust-dried track.

It was a relief to reach the village at last, when she was able to get out of the vehicle and ease her aching muscles. She stood looking around her, trying to imprint the scene for one last time indelibly in her brain.

Children had already started to appear, drawn as if by magic to the truck, climbing all over it, grinning, as Dave began to unload the equipment. As Georgia unfolded the small table, he spoke rapidly to one of the women who had gathered round—or at first glance Georgia took her to be a woman. Closer study of the lovely features told her that, despite the child she carried on her hip, she was probably no more than fourteen. The girl's face was anxious as she nodded, the beads in her hair jingling, her hands gesturing expressively in the direction of one of the huts.

'What is she saying?' Georgia began to lay out the equipment.

'Her husband is ill. It sounds like a head injury, possibly concussion.' Handing out the last of the bags from the back of the truck, he said, 'Do you want me to take it?'

'Would you? I'll make a start on the vaccinations and routine cases. I'll set up over there, by those huts. At least it will give us a bit of shade.'

They worked steadily through the morning, and at first she was too involved in what she was doing to be conscious of the sun rising higher in the sky, until she straightened up, trying to ignore the incessant throbbing in her shoulders.

Completing a vaccination and handing the protesting child back to its mother, Dave looked up and grinned. 'OK?'

'Fine. Or at least I will be once I've had a cold shower.'

'I was thinking more in terms of a cold beer myself.'

She groaned. 'Sadist.'

The next patient came forward, hobbling on a pair of improvised crutches, and she found herself wincing at the sight of a knee swollen by acute rheumatoid arthritis. She didn't need to question the man to know that he was in severe pain. His symptoms were typical—he moved with difficulty, he had a fever and was lethargic, probably as a result of the anaemia which so often accompanied the disease.

Georgia found herself having to stifle a feeling

of resentment that she wasn't able to prescribe all the things she knew he so desperately needed and which would have been readily available back in England: fresh milk, eggs and fruit, extra vitamins, all the things with a high energy value. As it was, she tipped prednisolone tablets into a container, doing her best to explain how they should be taken.

In the course of an hour they had dealt with the kinds of conditions they expected routinely to see. Infected wounds, septic teeth, a baby with the first signs of trachoma—the eye disease which was pitifully all too prevalent.

She looked at the watering stickiness of a child's eyes and felt her heart sink. He couldn't be more than six, yet the condition was already well advanced, showing a degree of scarring and corneal opacity which only surgery could put right.

'I shall need to see the rest of your family,' Georgia explained painstakingly to the man, who beckoned forward his wife and two more children, one a baby of just a few weeks old. Having completed her examination, she said, 'I am going to give you some medicine.' She took out a bottle of tetracycline drops. 'I want you all to use these, twice a day for three months.' By means of gestures she indicated how the drops were to be instilled. 'I'm also giving you some tablets.' She shook a supply of sulphonamide into a container, handing it to the woman. 'In time, your son will need to go into hospital, so that his eyes can be made better. In the meantime you must all clean your eyes carefully, every day, particularly your baby's eyes.'

Minutes later, watching them leave, she stifled a sigh as she began to dispose of soiled dressings and put the used instruments into a pan to be sterilised.

'Having trouble?' Dave completed his notes and looked up.

She sighed. 'Don't you ever get just the tiniest bit discouraged? Feel as if you're pouring water into a bottomless bucket? We hand out the pills and offer advice, most of which you know damn well is probably forgotten or ignored the minute we leave.'

He smiled wryly. 'You have to tell yourself that if one per cent of it gets through and has some effect, then you've achieved something.'

'We need trachoma clinics. . .'

'I agree,' he said evenly. 'And in some places it's beginning to happen. In the meantime we go on doing what we do, giving out the pills and the advice, as you say, and prodding the powers that be.'

'And waiting for a miracle.'

'That's the way it goes.' Grinning, he went back to work and she turned to her next patient, a woman with a nasty abscess which needed to be drained.

It was late afternoon by the time they had finally finished. Collecting used syringes and dressings, packing everything into the proper containers, Georgia paused to brush a hand wearily through her hair. 'That was quite a day.' She felt drained as she climbed into the truck and helped herself to a refreshing drink from the flask.

'Great idea.' Dave flopped into the seat beside her, gratefully accepting the refilled cup she proffered, pouring a little of the water over his face and neck. 'How did it go?'

'Fine. Vaccinations all complete. Everything else pretty much routine.'

He handed back the cup and looked at his watch. 'Time's getting on.' He frowned slightly as he put the truck into gear, moving slowly through the crowd of cheering children. 'We're going to be lucky if we make it back before dark.'

She shot him a look. 'Is that going to be a problem?'

He concentrated on the track ahead, grunting as the wheels hit a rut, then he smiled. 'No, I shouldn't think so. It just means you'll have to put up with my driving for a while longer, that's all.'

Laughing, she closed her eyes, just for five minutes to recharge her batteries. Half an hour later she was wakened by Dave's hand on her arm, shaking her roughly.

'What. . .?' Still half asleep, she struggled upright, to the realisation that they were moving fast. She stared into the darkness. 'What's happening?'

'We've got company. For God's sake keep your head down and hang on,' Dave ground out.

Georgia's knuckles were white as she flung out a hand to steady herself against the dashboard. Dave was concentrating on keeping as steady a course as possible over the almost non-existent track ahead.

'What sort of company?'

He shot a quick look in her direction. 'It has to be the local *shifta*. I spotted them about ten minutes ago.'

'Oh, my. . .'

'Are you all right?'

She felt the colour drain from her face as the chill of fear swept over her, but her reply was lost as the sharp crack of a rifle took her by surprise.

'Jeez!' Dave swore graphically. 'They're shooting at us.'

Georgia watched helplessly, feeling the dryness of fear in her throat as he tried to steer the truck with one hand, fumbling with the radio with the other. He swore again as the truck juddered against a rock.

'What are you going to do?'

'I'm not stopping, that's for sure. Hang on tight. I'm going to put my foot down.'

She hung on, bracing her feet. 'But why are they after us?'

'They probably think we're carrying supplies. *Hell*!'

Georgia swung round, crying out sharply as she saw him clamp a hand over his left arm and blood seeped through his fingers. 'You've been hit!'

He sucked in a breath. Georgia was on her knees trying to stem the flow of blood from his shoulder. Her heart was hammering. They were hurtling along, swinging precariously as Dave tried to steer with one hand on the wheel.

'Don't worry about me. It's a graze.'

She knew he was lying. 'You're bleeding too much.'

'Just find me something to press over it then grab the radio. Try to get through to base. Let them know what's happening and give a rough position.'

Just in case we don't make it, she silently added the unspoken words. With shaking hands she retrieved the radio, hanging on as the truck swayed again, sending her lurching towards him. She heard him cry out.

'Rover One to Batandi Base. Come in, Batandi. This is Rover One. Come in. . .'

'Reception may not be too good.'

Oh, my God, we could die out here, she thought. 'Batandi Base, come in, *please*. This is Rover One. We have an emergency. Come in, Batandi.' The radio crackled. 'It's no good; they're not answering.'

'Keep trying.'

She flung a look at him. 'You're still losing a lot of blood.'

He grinned weakly. 'Don't worry. I'm as tough as old boots.' But one look at his face was enough to tell her that he was in considerable pain.

With a renewed sense of urgency she tried again. 'Batandi Base, this is Rover One. Come in. Sam, where are you?' Her voice broke. 'Dave is hurt.' Her gaze flickered in his direction again and this time she felt a real prickle of alarm. He was swaying and his face was drained of colour. She stifled a scream as another shot rang out. 'Dear God. . . Come in, somebody, please.' Her voice was little more than a whisper; the words seemed to have been frozen by fear in her throat. The radio crackled again insistently.

'Hello, Rover One, this is Batandi. What did you say? Damn this reception.'

'Sam?'

'Georgia. I can hear you. For God's sake speak clearly. Where are you?'

'I'm. . .not sure. We left the village about half an hour ago. We've been shot at. Dave is hurt; he's losing a lot of blood.'

For one terrifying moment she thought he had gone as silence hung between them. Sweat trickled down her face. 'Sam, can you hear me?' Her voice broke in a sob of fear and she almost laughed when he spoke again.

'I can hear you. Don't lose your nerve, my darling, not now.' She realised he had been speaking to her all the time and she hadn't been aware of it. His voice was tense. 'Keep moving, for heaven's sake. I'll get to you as soon as I can.'

'I don't think we can. Dave. . .'

'I know. Just keep going, darling. For pity's sake, keep going somehow.'

She gave an involuntary sob. He had called her darling. It had all been part of the panic, of course, she knew that, but for some reason her heart was pounding crazily. 'I don't know where we are.'

His voice was suddenly strangely cool. 'I'll find you. Save your breath and hold on.'

The radio went dead; for a moment she stared at it. Terror had robbed the whole scene of any kind of reality. Her reactions were all purely instinctive now.

She saw Dave slump forward. The scream started in her throat but got no further. The truck grated savagely against a rock, rising against it, and then the whole world seemed to tilt. She was falling. Somewhere far away she heard Sam's voice calling out urgently. She felt a sharp blow against her temple then she plunged into blackness.

CHAPTER TEN

SOMEONE was bathing her face with water. It was deliciously cool and she moaned softly, not wanting it to stop.

'Georgia, for God's sake open your eyes. Say something. Look at me.'

She listened to the voice, angrily resenting its intrusion into her consciousness, and even more so the hands which, though blissfully gentle, persisted in probing areas of pain of which she was slowly, miserably, becoming all too aware.

'I don't think there's any serious damage. It's a miracle you weren't killed. A small injection. . . Open your eyes, Georgia.'

She obeyed, slowly, carefully, feeling as if she was waking from a drugged sleep, then a blurred face was bending lower, so close that it was almost touching hers, and she closed them again quickly. Her head ached and her hand rose to probe the spot, only to find a cloth pressed over it and someone else's hand.

'Sam?' Memory returned and she began to tremble so violently that her teeth shook. 'The truck. . .'

'Take it easy. You're safe. I've got you.'

179

'Dave. . .'

'He's going to be OK. He was flung clear as the truck turned over. He's got a nasty case of concussion and we had to dig the bullet out of his arm, but apart from that he's fine.'

She lay for a few seconds with her eyes closed, trying to shake the fuzziness that seemed to be clouding her brain. 'How. . .?' She licked her dry lips. 'How did you find us?'

'We just drove along the road we knew you must have taken. By some miracle the lights of the truck must have stayed on when it rolled.' His voice was taut and for the first time she looked at him clearly. His face was ashen and grim as she had never seen it before as he looked down at her. 'I thought. . .' A nerve pulsed in his throat. 'I thought you were dead. I heard you scream then the radio. . .'

Suddenly she was in his arms, sobbing as he held her close. As if in a dream she felt his lips brush against her hair, then her face, and she clung to him, feeling the weak tears coursing down her cheeks and able to do absolutely nothing about them.

'I'm sorry.' He released her slowly, resting her against the pillows. His voice was so soft, so gentle that she scarcely heard it above the dull drumming in her head. 'I don't think you're ready for this just yet.' He smiled and she wondered why everything was spinning round. It was like being sucked into a whirlpool, and she sighed fretfully, reaching out for his hand. His fingers closed strongly, securely over hers and she closed her eyes.

'Am I going to die?'

He laughed softly, but his voice was strangely taut. 'Not if I have anything to do with it. You have concussion. You had a nasty crack on the head and by morning I expect you'll have bruises in places you didn't even know you had. You were damn lucky,' he said tightly. 'When I think what might have happened.'

'Don't, Sam,' she said weakly, frowning as memory began slowly to return. 'The *shifta*, they were after us. . .'

'They probably guessed help was on its way. You weren't carrying any supplies, and they would have realised that as soon as they got anywhere near the truck.' His mouth tightened. 'They probably realised you were from the hospital. We help their families. It's not in their interests to make enemies of us.' He bent to brush a hand against her cheek. His voice faltered. 'You need to get some rest. I've given you an injection that should help you to sleep.'

'Sam. . .'

He shook his head. 'Go to sleep now. We can talk later. We've got all the time in the world.'

But have we, Sam? she thought as she tucked a hand under her cheek and fell asleep.

When she woke again it was daylight and she was in her own bed. Her head ached and Sam had been right about the bruises—they had come out with a vengeance. Otherwise, she realised, she was remarkably unscathed. Someone had left a Thermos of juice by her bed. She drank it greedily, surprised to discover how thirsty she was.

She lay for a while, dozing in and out of a strange state of lethargy until Jan tapped at the door and came in.

'Hi, I've come to see the invalid. How's things?' Surveying the bruises with professional interest, she winced. 'Ouch! That looks nasty, though from what I hear you were remarkably lucky.'

Georgia managed a short laugh. 'So they tell me.' More seriously, she said, 'How's Dave?'

'Feeling sorry for himself, not without good cause, I might add. His arm is going to be sore for a while and he's got the mother of all headaches, but he's going to be fine.'

'I must go and see him, to thank him.'

'Are you sure you feel up to it?'

'I'm fine, really. I couldn't do a cartwheel, but I'd feel a fraud if I stayed in bed.'

'Well, just take it easy. Look, I'd better get back. I'll see you later. Oh, and Sam says not to worry about a thing. They're managing nicely without you, so take all the time you need.' With a grin she was gone and Georgia sat gingerly on the edge of the bed, wondering why she didn't feel reassured.

Managing, with difficulty, to take a shower, she spent what seemed to be forever struggling into a pair of jeans and a T-shirt. She purposely left her hair loose. She knew from the single glance she had stolen in the mirror that she looked pale and drained. Her eyes were dark-ringed and she felt too bruised to apply even a light covering of make-up.

When she finally made it to Dave's room, he was sitting on the edge of his bed. He was dressed, and his injured arm was covered by a padded dressing. He looked up, smiling, as she tapped at the door.

'Can I come in?'

'Someone to talk to! I was just beginning to think I'll go crazy if I don't get out of here soon.'

She laughed. 'I know the feeling. They say doctors always make the worst kind of patient. How's the arm?'

He cocked an eyebrow. 'Still hanging on in there.'

'Idiot.' Her expression became serious. 'I want to thank you.'

'Hey.' He held up a hand. 'There's no need.'

'I mean it. If you hadn't reacted as you did, we might not have got out of there alive.'

He gave a wry smile and rose gingerly to his feet. 'I don't mind admitting it's not an experience

I'd care to repeat. We were lucky.'

'Will you still be able to fly?'

'What, with this? Hey, ma'am, have you never heard the saying on a wing and a prayer? Well, I got the wing. . .' He struggled to slip his watch on to his good hand. She went to help him.

'So you'll still be flying out tomorrow?'

'Sure. Sam says business as usual and we need those supplies.'

She said quietly, 'In that case I'd better make sure I'm ready in time.'

He stared at her. 'You're not still thinking of leaving? Heck! Surely things have changed?'

'Have they?' she said quietly. 'There's only one person can answer that.'

'So, go talk to the man.'

She shook her head. 'Sam has to want to let go of the past. I don't think he's ready. He was badly hurt; the scars are too deep. Maybe they'll never heal.'

Dave held her hand, stroking it with his thumb. 'You're in love with the guy.'

She met his gaze directly. 'I don't quite know how I'm going to live without him.' Her lips quivered and she turned away. She heard Dave swear softly under his breath, then he put his good arm round her and she rested her head on his shoulder, gulping hard until, with an effort, she pulled herself together and blew her nose hard. 'I'll get over it.' Some day, a hundred years from now. She forced a smile. 'But I have to leave. You do see that?'

Dave's mouth tightened, then he let out a sigh. 'Sure. I guess I'd do the same.'

She reached up to kiss his cheek. He pulled her towards him and kissed her properly, firmly, on the mouth. 'Some people don't know when they're well-off,' he growled.

Georgia would have laughed if she hadn't felt so much like crying.

She purposely avoided the hospital. Coffee and a couple of aspirins had lessened the headache, but she didn't want to see Sam, to have all her resolutions upset. If she stayed it would have to be for the right reasons, not for Sam's reasons. The time for compromising was over and, anyway, it had all been one-sided. Well, she couldn't live the rest of her life like that, playing second-best to the ghosts in Sam's past.

Her suitcase was open on the bed and she was emptying the small wardrobe, folding her clothes into the case. She supposed it wouldn't be too difficult to find another job when she got back home. She was qualified, good at what she did, yet suddenly she knew she couldn't go back and just pick up where she had left off, as if nothing had happened. She would have to make a completely fresh start, somewhere where there wouldn't be any reminders. If such a place existed.

She dropped a pair of shoes into the suitcase and was folding one of her white coats when the door was flung open.

Startled, she looked up. Sam was standing there, his expression darkening as he watched her.

'What the hell is going on? What are you doing?'

Her heart hammered in her chest. It needed a supreme effort of will not to stop what she was doing but, somehow, she managed to continue her packing without looking up. 'I would have thought that was fairly obvious.'

'You're packing!' His voice was incredulous.

She moved to the chest of drawers, took out a pile of shirts and began to fold them methodically. 'I thought I'd better make a start. It's a long trip. I want to be ready. . .'

He took a step into the room, looking around him as if suddenly bewildered. 'You're leaving?' He raked a hand through his hair. 'But I thought. . .'

Georgia met his gaze with a level stare, unwilling to allow herself to believe what she thought she saw in his face.

'I'm leaving with Dave tomorrow as planned. That was the arrangement. I see no reason to change it.' She glanced round the room, spotted a small photograph, and added it to the rest of her things.

Sam gave an oddly shaky sigh. 'What are you going to do?'

'I'm not sure yet.' She took her books from the shelf, smoothing the bindings. 'I'm booked on a flight out of Addis tomorrow afternoon. When I get home. . .' she shrugged '. . .I don't know. There are a number of options. General practice maybe.' She looked at him. 'Why the sudden interest, Sam?'

He stared at her, his throat working. 'I do care.'

'I know.' She had to look away. 'But it's not enough any more, not for me.' Blinking hard, she forced herself to look at him. 'I thought it was. I told myself I'd take whatever was on offer, but now I know I can't. It isn't enough, Sam. It took me a while to realise it. . .'

He had moved closer. He looked haggard; his face was pale. 'I've come to realise a few things myself in the past few hours,' he rasped. 'Not least that I almost lost you.'

'But you didn't, Sam.' She swallowed hard. 'I'm fine. Nothing's changed.'

'Damn it!' He grabbed her arms, glaring down at her. 'Of course it has. Everything has changed. Don't you see that?'

The unexpected contact almost broke the frail reserve of strength she was using to fight him. She could feel the warmth of his body, the pressure of his fingers on her skin.

'No, I'm afraid I don't.'

'We have to talk.'

Her head went back as she looked at him. 'There's no point, Sam. I don't think we have anything more to say.'

'You don't have to go. Georgia, please. I'm asking you to stay. I want you to stay.'

She closed her eyes, wanting an end to the torment. It would be so easy to give in, to accept him on his terms. 'Why?' she said bitterly. 'Tell me why I should stay, Sam.'

He stared at her. 'Because I'm asking you. Because I want you. Because I *need* you.'

'It's not enough, Sam.' Georgia shook her head. 'I wish it were, but it isn't.' She broke away and began to fold another blouse.

'If I say I love you?' His voice was ragged and uneven. Her hands froze. She willed herself not to turn around, knowing that if she did she would end up in his arms.

'Is that what you're saying, Sam?'

He reached out for her again, his voice unsteady, strangely vulnerable. 'It's what I feel.' He gave a deep, jerky sigh. 'When I thought I'd lost you, I knew I didn't want to live, that my life would have no meaning without you. I may have tried to deny it, but I do love you,' he said huskily.

She was trembling as she stared up at him. 'You know what you're saying? I won't compromise, Sam. It has to be all or nothing. Loving someone means trusting them. I give you my word, I won't ever hurt you, but if you doubt that, then don't say another word, Sam, because I couldn't bear it. . .'

He pressed a finger to her lips, then bent his head to kiss her. 'Can you ever forgive me for the things I said? For the things I did——?' He broke off, his breathing ragged.

Georgia hesitated. 'As far as I'm concerned, marriage means the whole package, Sam. Babies, sleepless nights, being a family.'

His eyes glittered. 'Is that an invitation, Dr Maxwell?'

She buried her face in his chest. 'It's a long-term contract, Dr Ryker. No get-out clauses, no time off for good behaviour.'

He gave a deep-throated rumble of laughter. 'No Brownie points if I'm exceptionally good?'

She looked up at him and smiled. 'Oh, I'm sure we could arrange something.'

He bent his head to kiss her again. 'I do love you.' His voice was soft and gentle. 'Marry me, Georgia. Marry me soon.'

She reached up to cup his face in her hands, pulling him down to return his kiss. 'Yes,' she breathed. 'Yes, please, my love.'

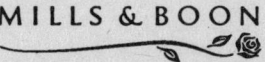

Look out for Temptation's bright, new, stylish covers...

They're Terrifically Tempting!

We're sure you'll love the new raspberry-coloured Temptation books—our brand new look from December.

Temptation romances are still as passionate and fun-loving as ever and they're on sale now!

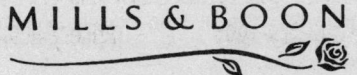

MILLS & BOON

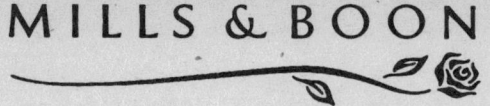

MILLS & BOON

CHAPTER ONE

GEORGIA MAXWELL woke slowly, shivering in the cold of an African dawn. Her mouth felt dry and, for a few seconds, as she jerked fully back to consciousness, she couldn't remember where she was.

A brief glance at her watch showed that she must have slept for nearly an hour. Blinking hard, she turned stiffly to look out of the window just as the small plane banked sharply over the deep rift-valley below. Then she remembered, gasping involuntarily as the thin veil of early morning mist broke and she caught her first real glimpse of the beauty below.

So this was Ethiopia, spread like the wings of a giant butterfly, caught and held between Sudan to the north and the desert plains of Kenya to the east.

She jumped as the pilot leaned across, resting a hand on her arm. Grinning, Dave Farrell raised his voice to make himself heard above the noise of the engines.

'It seemed a shame to wake you. You were sleeping like a baby. We'll be coming in to land in about ten minutes.' He nodded in the direction of the ground where sunlight shimmered on the surface of the water. 'I figured you'd want to take a look. You'll see quite a few lakes in this area. Some of them are fresh water, others brackish, depending on the source.'

Tucking a strand of honey-blonde hair behind her ear, Georgia gazed down at the scene below and felt her pulse-rate quicken as the rays of the fast rising sun ignited the slopes with the colour of molten gold. Seen from the air the vastness of the continent and its infinite variations, the change from arid desert to lush green slopes, falling away to the valley floor, filled her with a sense of excitement that banished every last scrap of tiredness.

Craning her neck, she said, 'I can see a river.'

Dave followed the direction of her gaze and nodded. 'That'll be the Awash. It runs north along the rift until it peters out in a salt lake somewhere on the plain.'

She nodded, staring out of the window as the ground seemed gradually to come closer, feeling her body respond with a sudden surge of adrenalin.

Not that she was a stranger to travel. It was in her blood. As a child whose father had been an army surgeon, she had developed a feeling of wanderlust at an early age, had been given the opportunity to see places most people only ever dreamed about. But never Africa.